Blind

AMINA HAQUE SOHRAWARDY

ISBN: 0692876839
ISBN 13: 9780692876831

Dedicated to my late father, Naim Uddin Haque, a lawyer. At a time when the world only strove for sons, he briefly and effectively raised his only child and daughter, to strive for more.

1

Sheila Scott lay in bed thinking about her past. She'd had many ups and downs in her life, and now she was going to be married. It was hard to decide whom she loved more, her parents or Richard. *I guess both; my family is everything to me*, she thought. *But Richard, who's going to be my partner for life…I can't imagine a life without him.*

She would not make the same mistake her parents had made. They had suffered through four years without each other and had gone through all those problems. It was just a little misunderstanding; pride and lots of anger had them separated for that long.

She was thinking about how much she wanted to be a lawyer—a good and famous one. She wanted to do something good with her life. She'd always hated the idea of working someplace for someone else. But she couldn't be a lawyer; she'd only just finished high school. The only other thing she could do…she shivered to think about it. She closed her eyes and rolled over so she could get some sleep. But thoughts kept coming. She remembered vividly the night when Mom and Dad had the big fight.

Mom and Dad had their differences. They loved each other, they told each other everything, but they had disagreements. They would start debating, and sometimes their debates would become arguments.

Most of the time, they compromised (mostly Mom gave in). But this time, the argument escalated even more. They were so angry, so rude, and so sarcastic. Mom started crying. Dad kept yelling and screaming. It sounded like he was talking to himself. Whatever anger he had inside he wanted to take it out. He shouted again.

"This is my house! I'll decide what you should do, Anna!" he bellowed, pointing at her.

"Oh! So this is only your house?" she asked, turning her face toward him. "Only yours?"

"Yes!" he shouted. "I've worked hard all my life, all the time, and I'm the breadwinner of this house. This is my house, and my decision is final!"

Mom didn't answer. She got up slowly from the corner of the bed where she was sitting as she came in her room at first to talk to her husband Scott, and deep in thought. She went to the desk, which was on the other side by the window in their room; mostly Mom used it whenever she wanted to do some writing and reading. She did not have to go the library this way; she could simply go to the desk in her room. She went there quietly and wrote a long letter on a piece of stationery. Then she packed some things in a small tote bag and made turn toward the door with pride. She did all this with tears in her eyes. Mr. Scott didn't pay any attention and went to freshen up. When he came out after refreshing, he saw Anna was going with her tote bag and pocket book towards the door where Sheila was standing.

Mom looked ill and tired. She moved very slowly toward her daughter. Sheila used to hear their debates time after time, but this was very different. She came at the door and stood there, frightened and sad. She knew something was happening, something big.

Mom and Sheila clung to each other. Mom was crying. Sheila screamed, "Mommy, don't leave me, please! I want to go, too! Mommy, take me, too, please! Mommy! Please!"

A hand came toward the girl, separated her from her mother.

"You're mine; no one can take you from me! Do you understand?"

It was dad; his face was red with anger. He told Mom, "You want to do that, get away from us? Go—right now. Just make sure you never come back—never!" He held his daughter's hand and pulled her close to him.

Sheila was confused, scared, and sad. She tried to grab the letter Mom had written, but Dad snatched it from the desk before she could and ripped it into four pieces.

"Dad!" Sheila screamed again, bending down to pick up those pieces from the floor. She kept them in her hand behind her back and looked at him, scared. He paid no attention to her picking up and trying to hide the torn-up letter from him; he was blind with rage.

He held Sheila's other arm tight for a long time, but she was more worried about the paper. She couldn't speak.

Sheila's mother left without even taking the tote bag. She was so angry and hurt that she just grabbed her purse and rushed out. Sheila cried. *Maybe Mommy is crying, too*, Sheila thought.

That was the worst night of Sheila's life. She couldn't sleep afterward. She was worried, scared, and sad for her mother. She was angry with her father but couldn't do anything. At first, she hoped that her mother would cool down and come back. But the more time passed, the more anxious she became. In the middle of the night, she heard footsteps. Could that be Mommy coming home? Was Daddy going out to look for her? She rushed out of her bedroom only to see Daddy in the kitchen, drinking a bottle of water. Sheila had nothing to say to him, so she returned to her room. The next morning she was exhausted, but her mental anguish overpowered her fatigue, and she got ready for school. She thought that maybe she would look around for her mother in the neighborhood instead of going to school. When she came out of her room, Daddy asked, "Where are you going?" He was similarly worried about his daughter. Even she was big enough to go to school by herself. She was a high school student. Still, her parents drove her to school in the morning when they went off to work.

"School," she replied, trying to avoid conversation.

"Let me take you," he said, equally terse.

As she waited for him, her eyes darted across the room. The air was very damp, the sky cloudy. The kitchen was dark. The house was quiet and still. Sheila's eyes filled with tears.

Daddy wasn't going to go to the office today, she thought. As Sheila waited for him to come out of his room, she worried that if she went to school, she would be stuck there and unable to look for her mother. She couldn't decide what to do.

Then the doorbell rang.

"Police!" a stern voice said from outside the front door.

"Daddy," she called to her father, "the police are here!" As Mr. Scott walked slowly to the door, she thought their visit might have something to do with her mother. Her heart beat fast. She was shaking and praying for good news. *Please, God, please.*

When Dad opened the door, two policemen were standing there. "Do you know this lady?" they showed a picture of her mother.

"Yes," Daddy said.

"May I know who she was?" one of the officers had asked?

"Mommy!" Sheila interrupted. "My mother, she's my mother. Where is she?"

The officers looked at her sadly. "Well, could you tell me why she was out walking at that time of night?"

A hand landed on her shoulder and pulled her back. Both officers just stood there, saying nothing. Finally, one of them said, "She was found—dead."

"What?" Sheila and her father both screamed.

The officers repeated the horrible news.

"She was found dead on the street, and her body is at the morgue. You can come and give us a report and make the identification, and then we can release the body."

Daddy listened calmly. When the police left, he held Sheila, and they both cried loudly. What happened next, she didn't know. She was shocked and sick. Her father was worried and sad.

For a while, life was very quiet. It was just Sheila and her father. He would come home at the same time every day. They both would go to the kitchen to fix something for dinner. They'd watch the news or some times another program. It was like a game or some show selected by Mr. Scott. Sometimes Daddy asked her about school, any problem or any homework she needed help with. "Thank you, Daddy. I don't need any help with my homework," she would answer. Conversation was sparse.

She always remembered her mother's arguments. And she never wanted to have that type of argument ever again in that house. She was enveloped by fear. Days passed and now they were used to the silence.

A couple of months later, she remembered that letter and could no longer ignore it. Her heart wished to put together the pieces of her mother's torn-up letter, to read whatever she had written and preserve that treasure in a safe place forever. *Oh God, where did I put it? I hope I didn't lose it. What am I going to do? Where should I look?* She asked herself.

She looked everywhere in her room. Then she started to panic. She tore her room apart. Tears welled in her eyes. Nobody was there to help, and no one came to look for her. No one wondered why she was in her room for so long. She cried as she tried to find those pieces.

Tap. Tap. She heard somebody coming closer to her room. She looked at her wristwatch. "Oh my God, it is so late!" she said aloud. Suddenly, a hand was on her shoulder.

"What's happening? What's this?" Her father's voice filled her ears. And she felt she was in her mother's shoes. Would he scream, yell, and kick her out of the house? She got so nervous and scared.

"Oh, Daddy, I'm sorry. I—I didn't realize the time."

"That's OK, honey. It's all right. But what's this?" Her father glanced around her room.

She didn't want to hide and didn't want to lie, so she said nothing.

After a pause, he looked at her and asked if she needed his help.

I wish, she thought, but all she could say was, "Thank you, Daddy. I'll find it later."

"All right, we can find it later," he agreed. "Let's go have dinner first." He turned and put one arm around her shoulders. They went to the kitchen. "Dinner is ready. Come on." Daddy walked around to the other side of the table.

"I'm sorry, I—I didn't realize about the time," she said again.

"That's all right, honey," he said and sat down at the table. "Remember that day I was busy and you prepared dinner?"

She nodded, still not looking at him. She was scared. *When he finds out what I'm looking for, he will be a different man. But what am I going to do if I don't find those pieces?* Her face revealed her feelings. But her father didn't want to bother her. Not while she was eating. Or maybe he had never seen her so puzzled.

"Shall we start?" He bent his head toward her with a little smile.

"Yes, of course." She put some food on her plate. *What was that?* She didn't want to know. The rest of the dinner was silent.

When they finished eating, they washed dishes and put the leftovers in the refrigerator. "Good night, Daddy," Sheila said. She wanted to go to her room and start looking again, but he stopped her.

"Wait a minute, honey. Let me help you. It's a big mess; you can't handle it alone." Mr. Scott started walking with her. Both of them went into the room. She didn't say what she was looking for. She looked here and there, very carefully. If she found those pieces of treasure, how would she explain it to him? She was in turmoil.

Mr. Scott was quiet, trying to hang up some clothes and stack some books. The room was quiet, except for the sound of footsteps and paper scrunching. "Was it a paper?" he asked.

"Yes. Did you find it, Daddy?" She forgot she was not going to mention the paper. She knew her father was very sensitive to this subject. They hardly talked about anything, which concerned her mother. But this time, she forgot. She couldn't help but show her eagerness. She turned to face him. He looked at her quizzically, with empty hands. His face was set, one eyebrow up, with a couple of lines creasing his forehead.

"It was a letter?" he asked again. He held a couple of books. Their eyes met; then she lowered her head, maybe because of fear. He put the books away and took a couple of steps toward her.

Oh God, what am I going to do? If I have to leave the house or he asks me to do so, where will I go? No, I'm not going anywhere. It is not going to happen. I'm not going to leave my house because of that letter. The letter was important to her, but being out on the street would be worse.

"Sorry, Daddy," she said, her head still down.

"You don't have to say sorry, honey," he said, coming to her. "Why didn't you tell me before? Why didn't you ask me about that? After all, you saved that. And you know what? You saved my life, too." He bent down a little toward her.

"What?" She looked at him.

He nodded his head. "Yes."

"How?" She looked at him, surprised. "How did I save your life?"

Mr. Scott stood still for a while, turned his head, and started to walk slowly around the room, disturbed. He took a deep breath and looked at her. She was still standing in the same place, still looking at him, very confused.

"When I was in the hospital to make arrangements for your mother's body, the police were there. They were asking so many questions. I don't remember what I said to them. All I know is, they refused to release her body. They told me to call a lawyer and wouldn't let me leave." He took a deep breath. "I called my lawyer. He came right away, and he asked me if I had any proof that she left behind, before leaving the house. Then I remembered that letter. I told him your mother had written a letter but I was so angry that I tore it up and threw it on the floor. He asked me if I threw the letter away. I told him no then remembered that you picked up the pieces from the floor. They came to search the house and found the pieces of the letter under your bed."

"Where was I?" Sheila asked. "How come I did not know anything about that?"

"You had a very high fever. I called the doctor, and he gave you some medicine. I had to leave while you were sleeping."

" Then what's happened, Daddy? I don't understand. Please explain it to me!"

He smiled. "About what?"

"That!"

"Why did I leave a sick girl alone?" He looked at her with a little smile.

"May I ask?" She looked at him, realized that her questions could make him angry, and then pictured the night she lost her mother. "That's OK, Daddy. We'll talk some other time."

"No, that's all right. I think you should know." He looked at her, and she got some encouragement.

"Well, what happened?"

"My lawyer is a very good man," he said. "He defended me. And that way I got your mother's body released." They both took a deep breath.

"Thank you, honey." He held her shoulders to pull her closer to him, but she didn't move.

Only God knows where she got the courage to ask, "What did you do with those pieces?"

"I saved them, with my personal documents. You can read the letter, if you want. I promise. Your mother is not in this world now. But it's important that the paper stays in a safe place."

"It's OK, Daddy. Thank you."

"Thank you! Now, let's start cleaning up this mess and get some sleep."

"Yes, sure," she said slowly.

"Any more questions?" Mr. Scott asked, guessing that something was on her mind. But she didn't answer. It no longer mattered what happened. All she knew was that her mother was gone and that she would still have that treasured paper.

The next morning the atmosphere was much lighter. *Maybe my mind is much clearer now*, she thought. When she went into the kitchen, Daddy was already there.

"Good morning," he greeted her.

"Good morning, Daddy. I think I slept late this morning."

"Actually, I woke up a little early," he said.

"Is everything all right?" Sheila asked.

"Yes, everything is all right. As a matter of fact, things are even getting better." He smiled a little.

Good, a short answer. They ate breakfast together. After finishing, she got up. "I have time to wash the dishes," she said.

"Thanks, and have a good day," he said and left.

Then one day her father came home with a lady. She was very pretty, nice, and pleasant. Sheila saw that her father, for the first time in a long time, was happy. He was laughing and talking like a regular person.

She is my very good friend Samantha and he told her that she was his only darling daughter Sheila.

All three had a nice dinner, which Daddy had ordered for home delivery.

Then Daddy and the nice lady went out. For the first time since her mother's death, Sheila stayed alone for a while. *It's OK. I can handle it.* He was happy and in a good mood, too. Why not?

Whatever had happened to my mother, it was a sad memory, and now Daddy was happy again. When he came back, they had a good conversation. He wanted to marry the nice woman. "She will be a good mother, Sheila. I have been observing her for a long time, and we had talked about all the ups and downs, too. I think she's the perfect person to take your mother's place, honey." He didn't wait for his daughter to give an answer. He stood up, stretched, then walked Sheila to her room, as usual, and went into his.

Sheila couldn't sleep for a long time; she remembered her mother. Everything was playing like a movie in her mind. *No one can take Mommy's place.* She took a deep breath. *Daddy didn't ask about my feelings; he just informed me. On the other hand, he's very happy; I shouldn't interfere in his happiness.* All sorts of questions ran through her mind, but she eventually fell asleep.

"Sheila," a voice came in her ear as a hand touched her head. She didn't want to open her eyes. Daddy had been in her room for a long time, trying to wake her up. But she had to get up.

"Good morning, Daddy," she said sleepily.

"Good morning! Did you sleep well?" he asked, softly.

"Yes," she said, holding in her emotions and beginning to get out of bed. "I'll be ready in just a minute."

"I'll wait for you." Her father gave a short answer, too, but could see her misery in her face. *Must be her sleep is disturbed because of this new development*, he thought and left the room.

After breakfast, he mentioned marriage again; he was asking her opinion.

She smiled. "Yes, Daddy, of course! You should start your life again."

Her father held her, and she cried inside. "I'll never leave you, Sheila," his voice said in her ear very slowly.

"I know, Daddy," she answered, giving him a hug.

"Next week is the ceremony," he said with his head down. It seemed as if he was talking to himself.

"Good to hear that," she said.

Her father looked at her then bent his head down again.

"One more thing," he said then looked at her.

"Yes, Daddy," she said, politely.

"Robert and his family are arriving in a couple of days."

"In a couple of days?" she asked. "Here?"

"Yes, because—"

"Yes, Daddy, because of what?" She was a little excited—happy but confused. It had been so long since Mom died, and now Uncle Robert and his family were coming. *At least I won't be alone for all the new changes. With Uncle, Auntie, and my cousins, things will be easier to accept. I'll have a good time.*

Deep in thought, she said, "Because."

"Yes, because what, honey?" He looked at her, perplexed.

"Because the wedding is next week," she reminded him.

"Yes, next week!"

She took a deep breath and a sad smile came over her face. "I have a question, Daddy. May I ask?"

"Sure, honey, you can ask anything."

"Are any of Mom's relatives coming?"

He stayed quiet for a while. Then he said slowly, "I'm afraid I don't have the courage to tell them about it. But I promise, later I'll go myself and tell them."

She felt relieved.

"I think your decision is right, Daddy."

"Good—good to hear that you're growing up. You're very intelligent and mature, too," he said.

"Thanks."

"So I don't have to worry about the arrangements for Robert and his family?" he asked, looking at her.

"Not at all," she said and got up. "Have a good day, Daddy."

"So soon?" he asked, looking up at her.

"By the way, I have to buy a couple of things for myself, so we can leave a little bit early tomorrow."

"Yes, of course." *There's no use talking to him*, she thought. "May I go now?"

"What time is it now?" he asked.

"It's seven thirty." She saw him look at her wristwatch.

"Already?" he looked at his watch.

Sheila smiled and gave him a big hug. "You're happy, so happy, and I'm happy for you, Daddy." Tears were in her eyes.

"Not for me only—for us, honey, for us. This house is biting me without your mother. I want to change the atmosphere for us, Sheila." He got a little emotional. "I want to bring your mother home for you." He bent down to face her.

"I know, Daddy, I know…but…"

"But what? Honey, if you're not happy, I can cancel the whole deal." He stood up.

"No, I don't mean that." She looked at him. "I'd never want to do that."

"Then what's the problem?" he asked.

"Nothing, Daddy." She wanted to say that no one would ever take her mother's place. Never! But she did not say anything.

The wedding was very simple but elegant; the Bride particular looked astonishing. She was wearing a beautiful dress, while Sheila's father was in a dark suit. His brother Robert was there with him the whole time and Aunty Sara kept her full attention on Sheila and the guests. She became a very good host. Sheila had all the arrangements for her uncle, his wife, and her cousins. But she did not have the courage or experience for that wedding. Her cousins were very supportive with her. And somehow she managed to pass the time successfully. All their relatives and close friends came. Sheila had invited a couple of her friends, too. And that's how the new mother came into their home and lives.

Uncle Robert and his family attended the wedding but were very quiet—obviously missing Sheila's mother. They were encouraging to Sheila's father, but the day after the wedding, they wanted to leave. Sheila tried to persuade them to stay, but her Uncle and Auntie said no. They acknowledged that Mr. Scott and Sheila had suffered a deep shock with the death of Sheila's mother and that it would take time to adjust to the newcomer in the home. They said they wanted to give the new family time to adjust. They urged Sheila to keep in touch and said she could visit them whenever she was on break from school. Sheila promised to call them as soon as she had some days off.

The new mother was nice, polite, and helpful. But living all three in the same house was too much for her. When Uncle Robert was leaving with his family. Robert asked to his brother Scott. When are you going for your honeymoon? He replied immediately and said, "Not now". Then, he saw his new wife and had a break for a couple of seconds and said slowly, we will make plans later. Samantha didn't say anything, though she tried hard to bite her tongue, with a few retorts lines in her head. She was trying to change everything around the house, so that the new look in the house would change the atmosphere. Daddy was very happy, because she was a cooperative lady. Sheila was calm, and why not? At least she could have some peace of mind at home. Time was passing, and the environment was changing too. Soon Sheila noticed that her stepmother's behavior was changing. She didn't appreciate anything Sheila did. Sometimes she accused Sheila of things she didn't do. Daddy was quiet, which was the worst. That's the last thing Sheila wanted; she did not want him to be the same as he had been before.

One day at the table, they told Sheila that since she was big now, she should begin taking care of herself.

"Meaning?" she asked.

"Meaning, you're finishing high school, so now you should start working, and if you want, you can continue your education. But first you have to settle down on your own."

She couldn't believe it. Her father had vowed he would never leave her. She wanted to remind him about that promise, but before she could, he said, "Your mother is right, Sheila. You have to learn how to run your life on your own.

"You know, so many times I was wrong; you can see it throughout my life"—he took a deep breath—"and the result was that I lost your mother. I don't want to make the same mistake again. I have to listen to your new mother. I think she's right."

Sheila was stunned and speechless. But she had to face the facts. She would do what she had to; she wouldn't end up like her mother.

"I'll prove myself," she said. "I can do it. I'm a brave girl. I'll finish my education and I'll leave the house now—right now." Her pride had provoked her.

She and her parents both rose from the table. In silence, they went to their room, and Sheila walked to hers. She put some things in a suitcase, collected all the money she had saved, then called one of her best friend. She had never told anyone about her family problems, but now she had to, and she asked to stay with her friend for a couple of days.

Her friend Sandra, who was living on her own, immediately said yes. Sheila wrote a note for her father and left.

Sandra helped Sheila find a part-time job, and they started going to the same school. Sheila never went back home and never called her father. She just tried to keep herself busy. She started taking more and more classes.

Did she want to finish her education quickly, or was she just trying to keep herself busy? The more classes she took, the more money she needed. So she worked more hours. Sandra was a year older than Sheila, but they had grown up together, had gone to the same school, and now were in the same college. Sandra was adopted. Her mother was a very good and kindhearted woman. A single mother, she had raised Sandra beautifully and had provided her a wonderful education and environment. But her health was poor. After finishing high school, Sandra became responsible for her mother as well as herself. She worked full-time and went to college part-time. She moved to a smaller house so she could manage the expenses for herself and her mother. "She did a lot for me," Sandra said of her mother. "Now it's my turn." Sheila supported that. Both were working hard and trying to fulfill their responsibilities. Sandra and Sheila were in the same college, but their class times were different. Sheila attended class in the morning then went to work. Sandra worked all day then went to school. So they hardly saw each other. Whenever they were together, they tried to spend good time without pressure. The two girls went out together. Some time Jimmy joined them, and as always, tried to be good company. Sandra and her mother soon looked at Sheila as a member of their family. Sheila didn't want to impose on their hospitality, but whenever she mentioned moving out, they would not have it.

Sandra said, "Don't talk nonsense with me!" She got a little bitter. "Where will you go, on the street to die? We don't have any problem with you living here."

Sandra's mother hugged Sheila and asked, "Are you not comfortable here?"

"I'm more comfortable here than I was in my own house," Sheila said, "because I have peace of mind here. But how long I can live like this?"

"As long as you need," they said together. "We're fine."

"May I contribute some help in the household?" Sheila asked.

"Yes," Sandra said, very calmly.

"How?" Sheila looked at her with some encouragement.

"By keeping your education as it is. I have to leave now for work; I'm late. And no more conversation on this topic again, please."

"Thanks," was all Sheila could say, and she bent her head down to hide her tears. After that, she never mentioned leaving again.

One night, after she had lived with Sandra for a long time, the phone rang. She answered it and heard her father's voice. She had wanted to hear it for so long, but when she finally heard from him, she got so emotional and sad that she felt her head was spinning and his voice was coming so slow, and slower...

2

Roger Scott belonged to a respectable farm family, work-ing the acreage that had been handed down to his father. He had a happy family: his father; his mother; and his old-er brother, Robert Scott.

Robert was always involved in the farm business. He had an education, up to high school but he was not in-terested in going to college. He married Sara, a girl from another farm family, who was simple, honest, and family oriented. They had attended the same school then took some business courses after high school. Sara wanted to help her mother as her father had died when she was in high school. When she finished her schooling, she didn't want to leave her mother, who was a homemaker, and younger brother and little sister, who were still in school. Sara had grown up in an environment where women took care of the home and men worked to provide the income.

While relying on their husbands for money, women had the duty of running the household. That's the way Sara's mother grew up. She was a good hardworking woman. She had wisdom and a sense of humor. She was a very good friend of Robert's mother, and their children spent a lot of time together.

Mr. Scott was completely different. He finished his schooling and asked his father to send him to college. Their father was not an educated man, but he appreciated the value of education. He wanted both his sons to get an education then use what they had learned in his farming business. He knew that money and knowledge were necessary for business success. When he had started his business, he had taken a chance and used all his savings. Now he wanted to apply education and new techniques to his enterprise. Combining knowledge and hard work, he thought, would bring him more success. So he agreed to send Mr. Scott to college to ensure a bright future for the farm.

Mr. Scott was intelligent and an excellent student. Many colleges accepted him for admission, but because his mother's health was failing, his father was getting older, and Robert and Sara were always busy. He had wanted to be able to come home and help around the house while still receiving an education. His decision made everyone happy, especially his mother.

Time passed quickly, but when he was almost finished with college, his mother died, then his father. Mr. Scott grieved and felt very much alone. His brother, Robert, was also deep in sorrow, but he had his wife right beside him, and now he was the keeper of his father's dream, the business. The brothers were close and understood each other. When Mr. Scott was offered his share of the land, he told his brother. "Our parents are gone. I don't want to be a farmer. I want to go back to school. You're the one who puts in all the effort and hard work, so you should have the profits."

Mr. Scott went back to school, and while he was there, he met a girl named Anna, who was beautiful, educated, and smart. She also had a sense of humor. Mr. Scott was impressed with her, and they quickly became friends. After Mr. Scott earned his bachelor's degree and his master's in business administration, he accepted an offer for a very good job. He then took Anna to meet his brother and sister-in-law. They both liked Anna very much, and Mr. Scott had an idea form Robert and Sara if he wanted to marry Anna. Robert and Sara had their own judgment and decided to meet Anna's family, so she invited her sister and uncle to come to town. This was when Mr. Scott realized that Anna did not have parents. Suddenly, it became clear why she spent most of her time at school, working, or studying. He had noticed she was quiet and that she kept busy and was careful about the people she befriended. She had many passions, as well as good judgment. She and Mr. Scott were very much alike. They became good friends and soon fell in love. They spent all their time together. When Mr. Scott finished school, he told his brother that he was moving to another state for his job. He said he was planning to get marry and start a family. When Robert asked if he had anyone in mind for his wife, even he had an idea that his brother loved Anna. Mr. Scott thought only of Anna too but he wanted to make sure with her first. He told his brother that he would let him know in a few days.

When Mr. Scott saw Anna, he told her he wanted to get married.

"I'm very happy for you," she said quietly, lowering her head.

He looked at her and smiled. "I'm very happy," he said.

"Meaning?" she asked with a little surprise.

"Are you seeing anyone?" he asked.

"You said you're getting married, right?"

"Yes, but you didn't ask with whom I want to marry."

"What difference does it make?"

"Will you marry me?" he asked.

She looked at him for a couple of seconds and, without saying a word, threw her arms around him. As they held each other, they said in unison, "I love you!" Then they both laughed. Anna smiled broadly as tears of joy welled in her eyes.

"Why are you crying?" Mr. Scott asked, bending toward her.

"I was so scared; I was so sad. I thought my world was ending. You know that I'm alone."

"You're not alone," Mr. Scott said. "You have me."

"Thanks," she said slowly. "In my family I don't have anyone except my sister, who's a lot older than me. After I lost my parents, my sister didn't marry until I finished high school. She didn't want me to feel like I was alone. I have an uncle and a couple of cousins."

"Good to hear that. We'll invite all of them."

Mr. Scott was thinking he wanted to end her sad story. He wanted to be the one to make her happy. He wanted them to be together and enjoy life.

"Robert and his family are excellent. I'm very impressed with them," Anna said.

"Thank you," Mr. Scott replied, lost in thought.

"Is something wrong?" Anna asked him.

"No, not at all. I just wanted to tell you about my father's will," he said. "I mean, what he left for us—me and my brother, Robert."

"Yes, what's happened?" she asked with a hint of concern in her voice.

"I was always involved in getting my education, and I offered very little help to my father with his land and his business. My father sent my brother and me to school, then I went to college and Robert went for business classes. He was very interested in my father's land and business. Since my parents' deaths, he has devoted himself to Daddy's farm and business. His wife was always with him. They have two children, and I love my niece and nephew very much. My brother and his wife are very honest and very loyal people. Robert has helped me get an education by never complaining about having to handle the farm and the business without help from me. Now he wants to give me half, which is my share. But I refuse to take that. The farm and the business belong to my brother and his family.

Even when he was taking his class, Robert worked with my father. He chose a business school close to home so he could work after class. He never skipped his classes; never failed a test—and he never let our father down. He deserves to have all the property."

"I'm happy to hear that," Anna said, "but why are you bringing up all this right now?"

Mr. Scott looked at her, smiled a little then said, "I want to tell you everything about my life."

"OK, but why now?"

"I want everything out in the open so you don't have objections later on," he said.

Anna paused, and then said calmly, "We're going to be married. Money, land, and all those things will never come between us—never."

"Promise?" Mr. Scott asked, looking relieved.

"Promise," she said. "We'll work hard and we'll make our own home."

Robert and his wife gave the couple a big wedding, a big home, and enough cash to get started. Mr. Scott didn't want to accept anything, but his brother insisted. "This is your share—only thirty percent," Robert said. "There's twenty percent more for you whenever you want it."

Mr. Scott said, "From now on, only thirty percent is mine. The seventy-percent share is yours, with my blessing."

Robert resisted: "Why? This is our father's land, and he inherited it from our forefathers. This is not only mine, Brother; this is ours—yours and mine."

"Only one problem," Mr. Scott said.

"What?" Robert asked. "What's the problem?"

"That you two are putting in all the effort, taking care of the business, taking care of this house *and* our father's and forefathers' home. You spent your life here, and you showed interest in all these things while I spent my life in the city, especially after our parent's death. I spent my life in my education. I got married to an educated girl who works mostly part-time, while your wife works all the time with you. This is the fruit of your labor, Brother. And if you don't accept that, I'll open an account for my niece and nephew, and my twenty-percent share will go to them.

Robert looked down then said slowly, "Thanks."

"You're welcome," Mr. Scott said. "And I want to make this legal, so in the future, no one can challenge this."

The brothers hugged tightly.

And that is how Mr. Scott and his brother, Robert, started their lives in such different ways. They remained close. In the summer, Robert and his family visited the city on vacation. In the wintertime, Mr. Scott took some time off work so the families could spend the holidays together.

Everyone had very busy lives, and time passed very quickly. Mr. Scott and Anna had a child. His brother Robert had two children, the children grew up, and everyone was fine, busy, and happy. Then suddenly life took a sharp turn. Anna disappeared and was found dead shortly afterward. Mr. Scott eventually remarried, and Sheila had all her problems.

After Anna's death, Robert and his family found out she had had an accident and died. He and his brother grew apart. The summer and holiday visits ended. Robert didn't know whether his brother's new wife was coming between them or whether his brother was distancing himself as he settled into a new life. Robert decided to wait and see. He stayed in touch with his brother with phone calls, but the conversations were short and simple. Robert was generally open, but Mr. Scott was a private person and kept things to himself. Sheila was private, like her father, but bold and open-minded, like her father's family. If she thought something was right, she would stand up for it and fight until she prevailed. She was very brave, determined, hard-working, and proud. She never wanted to be obligated to anyone. Even though she knew that Uncle Robert would gladly help and support her, she had no desire to ask him for help. She wanted to succeed on her own and prove to everyone, especially her father, that a person can achieve anything with good health, determination, and effort.

3

Sheila woke up in the morning and found herself in a hospital bed. A doctor was bending over her, saying, "Sheila… Sheila…wake up…please wake up…wake up." He looked worried as he pressed a stethoscope against her chest, checking her heart.

"I'm all right. Where am I?" She tried to get up, but he stopped her.

"Please don't try to get up."

"Why?" she asked.

"We'll explain it to you later," a nurse said softly. "Right now you need rest. OK, honey?"

Later in the morning, Sandra came in. She was worried and immediately started asking questions as she tried to rouse Sheila from her rest. "How are you feeling? Oh, you look so pale and weak. What happened to you yesterday? Who was on the phone? Tell me, Sheila! Please wake up!"

Sheila opened her eyes and looked at Sandra. Then burst out, "It was my father...my father. Oh, I hate him; yes, I do! I didn't want to talk to him. You believe me, right, Sandra?" Her face was now wet with tears.

"Yes, I do—I do. You're right about that." Sandra didn't want to hurt her. But she knew now why Sheila had fainted. At least she could tell Richard why she fainted. Sandra knew how much he worried about Sheila and how he felt about her. She only wished Sheila could feel the same way.

Two days later, Sheila told Dr. Richard she wanted to go home.

"Home?" Richard's eyes narrowed for a moment.

"I mean, where I live right now." Then she looked at him. "What difference does it make? I feel all right now, and I want to leave the hospital."

But Dr. Richard refused to discharge her. He told her that treatment should be completed; otherwise, the same thing could happen, and she would have to go through everything all over again.

"What do you mean by 'treatment'?" Sheila asked. "I don't understand. Please explain it to me! Do I have something dangerous?"

"Thank God, no, but we have to complete all the tests."

"Why?"

"This is the hospital's policy," he answered shortly.

"But I can't afford that expense!" Sheila exclaimed.

Dr. Richard's two gray eyes stayed on her for a while. His face was plain, but she felt he was hiding something. *He is trying to control some emotion*, she thought. At last he took a deep breath and picked up his stethoscope. "Sheila, I run this hospital. I'm the one who charges people or not." Then he gave her a quick glance. "I don't want anything from you." Just for her satisfaction, after a little pause, he said, "after all, you are Sandra's friend."

Oh, this man is so good, very handsome and graceful. How will I repay him for his kindness? She thought. *But no, I don't want anything to happen with me like my parents; it won't happen again, of course not. I have to be strong. I have to control my feelings, my heart, and myself. I have to, and I will.* She was about to say something, but he left the room.

Sandra came in, and Sheila burst out again, "Why did you admit me to the hospital? I was just in shock, not dying."

Sandra answered calmly, explaining how worried she had been. "I didn't know what was happening to you. I just called Dr. Richard, and he came right away and carried you to his car. He admitted you to the hospital and told me that it was nothing serious, so I could drop by the next morning. I was late for work, so I left." She stopped for a minute, looked at Sheila, then said quietly, "To be honest with you, I was completely satisfied after putting you in Richard's hands."

"Why?" Sheila asked. "Why did you call him? And why were you satisfied?" That's what I want to know."

Sandra was looking at her the whole time and listening; she knew about Richard's feelings, too, how he was impressed with her. And she knew also that no woman had ever impressed him before. But she held back, keeping quiet for a while, thinking, then looked at her and said, "He cares about you, Sheila, very much. Think about that."

"What?" Sheila was surprised and angry. "Who's he, and why does he care about me. Why?"

Because he is a doctor and we have known him for a long time. As a matter of fact this is the only doctor we know. And yes, he does care about you. We know that."

"But why? Who am I? Does he feel sorry for me? Because I come from nowhere, hanging in the air, so everybody feels sorry for me?" She took a breath. "And who is 'we'?"

Sandra lifted her head to face her. "Me and Jimmy."

"Oh, so he knows, too?"

"Yes, he's known for a long time."

"But I don't know him. I just saw him for the first time."

"Yes, because he was in medical school and living in the dorm. When he came back his father was ill, he got involved in the hospital and work. After all, he's a doctor, head of this hospital." She paused and then continued, "He's a very busy and a respectable man."

"So you had sympathy for him and left me here?"

"Yes, and I think you're crazy." Feeling aggravated, and before her answer, she picked up her pocketbook and left. Sheila was stern and emotional.

Somebody can love her, too Sheila was thinking. Dr. Richard came into the room on his regular round. He and Sheila looked at each other for a while. She was still in the hospital under Dr. Richard's supervision. Sheila stepped forward then suddenly stopped. She wanted to go to him, but she couldn't do that; she turned away and held the hospital chair handle very tight.

"Is something wrong, Sheila?" Richard asked softly.

"No…yes…you know, actually, I'm fine now. I feel fine, and I have to go somewhere badly, Doctor. Please let me go now." Her words rushed out, and she felt she wasn't making herself clear. She took a deep breath and looked up at him. She found a little smile on his face, a mocking one.

He took a step forward and said, "You said that you have to go somewhere. May I know where?"

Sheila looked at him sharply. She wanted to give him a stern answer, but she couldn't. "I don't want to discuss it. I have some personal things to do."

"Well, if I may say so, I know your personal things, too."

"Excuse me?"

"Sheila, I have an opening over here, right in this hospital, if you want to start."

"No!" she yelled, and then she thought of something. "You see, Doctor, I can't stay here."

"Why not?" Richard asked. "I think you should try."

"May I ask, how do you know that I need a job?"

"Oh, we have to get all of our patient's medical and personal information" Dr. Richard reply very calmly.

Now she understood his offer, *maybe he is feeling sorry for me*, she thought, but did not want to have a discussion on this topic.

"I have a job," she just said.

"Then maybe you're working too hard."

"I have other reasons, too."

"What reasons?" he asked again.

"I don't have any experience. I just finished high school, that's all. And I want to do everything myself. I don't want to be obligated, I don't Doc—"

"Richard," he said, interrupting her tirade, "my name is Richard, Sheila, and I'm a human being, not just a doctor."

Sheila looked at him. She was tempted to give up everything, accept his offer, and go on with her life quietly. But no, she couldn't do that. She needed to succeed on her own, without help from Sandra or Richard or anyone. Her brain was spinning. What should I do? She lowered her head and closed her eyes; for a minute she felt dizzy again.

"What's happening? Are you all right? Don't worry. I don't want to force anything on you. You're right to think about it, but please remember one thing. Whenever you need any help at all"—he raised his right hand—"I'm here. I promise you that." He turned to go, then stopped. "Oh, if you want to go home, you can, but I don't think that's a good idea. So let's finish the tests. Then you can decide for yourself."

"Thanks, Doctor! Very much."

He looked at her, smiled slightly, and then left.

Once again Sheila was in Sandra's house, worried about her job, college, and money. She was deep in thought when Sandra came into the room.

"Sheila, what are you thinking?" Sandra asked. "Are you feeling all right?"

"Yes," Sheila said.

"I'm going for shopping. Do you want to come with me?" Sandra asked.

"No, Sandra, you go ahead," Sheila answered.

"Why? Tomorrow we have to go for our next semester, and we'll be busy again. I want to have a good time today."

"Sandra, I have to look for a job," Sheila said slowly.

"Job? You just came back from the hospital! You're not going anywhere. Besides that, you have a job."

"I have to try to find something better than this job, more money, reasonable hours and close to my school. I cannot get all those conveniences without a struggle. Can't sit and get like that? Sheila stood up.

Sandra got up, too. "Dr. Richard just offered you a job."

"But I don't want that. I don't want to have any connection with him. I don't want any man's sympathy."

"That is not sympathy, Sheila. It's more than that believe me. He's not like that," Sandra tried to explain.

Sheila looked at her, and then spoke slowly, "I want to do it myself. I know I need a job badly. I know he's offering me one, and I can get it very easily. But I don't want that kind of sympathy. I want to try first. If I can't get one myself, I'll go back there."

"Is that a promise?" Sandra asked.

"Promise," Sheila said with a smile. "OK, let's go. I have to go too."

"With me?" Sandra looked at her with hope.

"I'm going to find some work," Sheila said.

Sheila walked all over for a couple of days but could not succeed.

She came back to Sandra's home. Felt a little tired, made a cup of coffee for herself, and sat on a chair in the corner of the room, quietly thinking.

Oh God, next week college is going to open. How will I start my education? How will I keep it going? What's going to happen to me? I have a job, but it's not enough for my tuition and personal expenses. That's why I want to have one more; even a part-time job should be enough, she was thinking. She thought about taking out a college loan, but she decided against it. *No, it will be too much to pay back. I should try to get by on what I can earn.* Then Sandra came in the room with Richard and Jim.

"Hello," Jim said to her. "How are you? I don't see you anymore!"

He tapped her on the shoulder. "How are you?"

Sheila was looking at Richard's face; he was looking at her, too, and his face was set. It looked as if he was feeling some kind of pressure. Then Sheila turned away toward Jim and Sandra.

"Richard, we're going to take a little walk," Jim said. "Would you like to come with us?"

Richard declined. "I'll wait for you here," he said. "I have to check on one of my patients."

Jim waved his hand, and he and Sandra both said, "bye" to both of them. They left, alone; Sheila and Richard were both quiet. Richard couldn't keep his eyes off her. He looked very graceful without his jacket, wearing black pant and a light blue-striped shirt open at the collar with the sleeves rolled up.

Sheila wanted to run away, but she couldn't. Her knees were weak, and her heart was pounding.

"Well, I'm your guest; won't you invite me to sit down?" Richard asked, moving in her direction. She remained silent, her eyes down. "Sheila, I came here to talk to you. Can we sit down, please?" He touched her shoulder lightly. "You have nothing to fear from me. I promise. C'mon, sit here." He walked with her to sit beside him. "Now tell me, how are you doing? How is your family and—"

Sheila looked at him quickly. "I don't have any family. I'm alone, Doctor."

"I'm here as a friend, not a doctor," Richard said.

"Oh, sorry."

"OK, apology accepted," he replied with a little smile. "Now tell me, how is your job hunting?"

"I didn't get anything yet," she said slowly. "I'm still looking."

"I thought you had one," he said.

"Yes, but I want to have a better and more convenient job so I can continue my education."

"I see," Richard said, taking a deep breath. "Did you take the admission exam?"

"Sandra made me take that, but I don't think I can keep taking classes this semester. Why are you asking?"

"Because I care about you—very much," he said quickly. His face was set. "I don't expect anything from you, Sheila—but a friendship. Just a good friend."

"Why me? I'm not important enough. You're a doctor. It makes no sense."

Richard looked at her deeply. "Why not? I'm nothing. I'm just starting out. I just finished school two years ago. This hospital was my father's. He died just last year. Since then, I've taken care of the place." He paused. "Of course, he trained me for a year. As soon as I finished college, my residency started at his hospital; he gave me full authority. First I was so bored and nervous and always used to complain to my father that I didn't want all this responsibility. But he didn't listen to me; it seemed like he knew what was going to happen to him. And after his death, I had to have all these responsibilities. Of course, Jim helped me a lot." He looked into her eyes.

She looked down.

"I've known you for a while," he said.

She looked up and met his gaze again.

"First when you came to Sandra's birthday party, then at her engagement, and a couple of times more, but you always seemed to avoid me. I thought you had someone in your life. I'm a busy person; I don't have time to chase after everyone. And then you were admitted to my hospital. Now, I know all about you.

"How do you know everything about me," she looked straight to his face.

"I told you, through your medical file, and Sandra too". He paused a little, and then said, "I told you, a doctor should have all the information about his patient".

She didn't say anything.

I am here with my friends and I want to be your friend also, Sheila. Can we be friends?" He extended his hand to her. "Just a friend—good company. C'mon, shake hands, and I promise you, I'll never turn my back on you." Richard's promise brought her father's words to mind: "I'll never leave you, Sheila." Her father had let her down, and now she was here. She wanted to tell Richard no, but she reached out and put her hand in his. Richard's face brightened. "Thanks, friend." Then he sat beside her and started talking about different topics just to break her hesitation; he asked what she liked and how she spent her days. How she was feeling and conversation was on for a long time when they realized that Sandra and Jim came back and noticed Sheila and Richard were talking and looked very happy, too. "Good luck, my friend," Jim said to Richard, and Sandra demanded to go somewhere on Richard's dime.

But Sheila was quite shy, happy, and scared. *Why did I do this?* She was thinking to herself. She knew how she felt about him. Could she stay as just his friend? Or would she want a lot more? And if she did, what would happen? Just like her parents…No she couldn't do that. *I'm going to tell him that I can't go on with this friendship. I'm not going to trust anyone. Not even him. But no, when I was shaking hands, he was so happy, and I was, too. No, that's not true!* She tried to hide her feelings from herself. *I can't. I'm not going to let happen to me what happened to my parents. But how can I control myself? He makes me happy. It's a different feeling when I see him—God help me.* She prayed at last.

"OK, let's go," said Jim. He held Sandra's hand and started walking.

Sheila wasn't ready to go and protested mildly, but they didn't listen to her.

"Please don't spoil my dinner. I'm starving," Jim pleaded.

They had a very good time. They went to a movie first, then a good restaurant, because Jim wanted that. "I don't have to pay today, so why worry, girls? Enjoy! Have a good dinner at Richard's expense."

They were all smiling, especially Richard. He appreciated their company. After dinner, Sandra had to buy something, so they went shopping, and afterwards, for a little walk.

"Oh, I'm very tired; I just want to go home and get some rest," said Jim. He always enjoyed things at first, and then later complained about being tired.

"All right, we'll stay just a little while longer," Richard, said.

"Wow, what's happened to Mr. Rock? He wants to spend more time outside."

"Do you know why?" Richard asked.

"I know, but you'll tell me anyway."

"Because I didn't receive any calls."

"I did." Jim was looking at him with an innocent expression.

"When?" Richard asked seriously.

"Just now, when we were walking."

"From where? I mean, which department?" Richard checked his cell phone again, and there was nothing. He looked toward Jimmy.

"From coffee, snacks, home, and bed," Jim said with his serious face. And all three laughed. Sheila didn't understand, but she laughed anyway.

"This is an emergency," Jim said. "Let's go."

"Where are we going?" Richard asked.

"To the girls' house, or we can take them to our homes."

"That would not be proper," Richard said softly. He was in a good mood, and Jim was taking advantage. Sandra listened to every word and kept smiling.

"Who's Mr. Rock?" Sheila asked Sandra very softly, but Jim heard.

"You don't know? You spent the whole day with Mr. Rock today," Jim said.

Richard didn't say anything, just bent his head with a little smile. Sandra looked at Sheila and winked.

"Today is a very lucky day," Richard said, glancing to the girls.

"And may I ask why?" Jim asked, smiling.

"Because the hospital hasn't called yet," he said, trying to change the subject.

"Wow! Congratulations." Jim laughed at last. It was very late when they arrived back at Sandra's home. Jim went with Sandra to make coffee for everyone. He always liked to make hot coffee. Sheila had no choice but to stay with Richard. She was quiet, trying to be busy, moving things from here to there. But her heart was beating very fast; her brain was not cooperating with her. She knew Richard was watching her every movement. Then she sensed he was walking across the room, and at last he came up behind her. "So, we're friends now." He looked at her deeply and smiled. "I hope you had a good time."

"Yes," she said slowly.

"Me too, I had an excellent time, I hope, we will have moor, he was looking at her. She just saw him, wanted to say some thing but the words refused to come out.

"I want to tell you that I'll never go back on my promise." We are just good friends.

Sheila looked at him. She could read the emotions on his face. She turned quickly as tears filled her eyes. She had always wanted to be loved by someone. But she couldn't get that. She lost her mother, and her father turned his back on her. Now him? Could she take that? What if he changed? *No, I can't think of that.* She turned her face toward him again.

"Are you crying?" Richard asked. "You don't trust me? All right, time will tell. Just promise me two things."

She looked at him.

Richard continued, "First, we'll always help each other, and second, we're not going to have any secrets between us. I'm promising that," he vowed, raising his hand. "Can you?"

She didn't know what was happening, but she felt her voice coming from her heart. Her hand raised, and she could only nod her head.

"Good!" Richard's voice came with a bright smile, and she blushed.

"Coffee is ready!" Jim and Sandra were coming. They had their coffee and little snacks because after dinner they had done a lot of walking. Jim started stretching, and although Richard wanted to stay longer, he was also tired. It was almost eleven o'clock. Sandra looked at her wristwatch and went to make sure her mother had eaten dinner and taken her medication. When she came back, both men were ready to leave. Sandra and Sheila said bye to both of them.

4

Time was passing rapidly, as usual. Sheila was in her second year of college. She and Richard were still good friends; he had kept his promise. Once he asked her to help in the hospital. She helped him, and he was very happy.

"You did very well, Sheila. Would you be willing to work here permanently?" Richard asked.

Now she was not afraid of him. Besides that, his behavior and manners were impeccable. The job was a good opportunity and close to her college, too.

"All right, but I can't work full-time, you know."

"I know." He put one hand on her shoulder. "That's my problem. I'll set your hours at your convenience."

From then on, she worked in the hospital. She was constantly looking for ways to help out, but it seemed that Richard's secretary, Julie, took care of most things. Once she complained to Richard, saying, "I feel like I have nothing to do here; Julie does everything. I feel like I'm being paid for doing nothing."

"Your being here is everything to me," he said.

She understood. But the change was that she didn't feel bad about it, and she wasn't scared, either. She felt very happy and secure.

But Richard felt uneasy. He always worried about her. Maybe she would change her mind about being his friend. It could happen. If she didn't like something, she might get angry. He knew her past had left psychological scars. She was insecure and needed to be loved. He wanted to give her everything. Her happiness and love were the most important things in his life. But he knew that winning her trust would be the hardest thing to do in his life.

"Do you have time for me to ask you something?" she asked slowly.

"Yes, of course. What is it?"

"Oh, nothing important. I was just wondering why you haven't married yet? I mean you should have a girlfriend at least. And that way your work will be easier, too."

"Being married?" He looked at her with surprise.

"Yes."

"How?"

"You would have your wife to help you, and you would have a companion, too." She looked very innocent and naïve.

"Why not you?" He was surprised and a little angry, and the words came out automatically.

"What?" Sheila's face turned red.

"Let's go for lunch." He changed his words. Richard couldn't understand if the redness of her face was from being shy or angry. They both got up.

"Let's go," she said in a normal voice.

But Richard sat again in the chair; he bent his head down, rubbing both hands.

"What's the matter? You look so serious," Sheila looked at his face. "Do you feel all right?"

"I just want to go home and get some rest. What do you want to do? May I drop you off somewhere?"

"I thought we were going for lunch."

"I have a headache," he snapped, and started walking.

His attitude had changed, so she decided not to talk anymore. "Yes, I have to turn in some papers at school, and I have a class. Then I'll be there."

"Where?" he asked.

"Your home. Don't you want me to come?" She smiled brightly.

"You're kidding. It will be a pleasure!" Richard was surprised; for a moment he forgot his headache. All this time and she had come to his house only twice. Once on his birthday, when they had celebrated with Jim, and another time with Sandra, but now! "See you." Richard didn't want to show his excitement.

About seven o'clock, when she had finished all her work, Sheila was at his door, as promised. She wanted to ask how he was feeling and find out what she should do in case he wouldn't be at the hospital the next day. But she could ask those things on the phone, too. *So why did I come here?* She asked herself. At the same time, her finger pressed the bell. His housekeeper answered the door and showed her to the living room. Jim was writing something. She walked toward him.

"Hello, Jim, what are you doing here?"

"Hey! What are you doing? I mean, you know that—I—I mean, Richard knows that you're coming?"

"Yes, why do you ask?"

Jim did not reply, just bent his head and started writing again.

"Where is he?" Sheila felt something was wrong. It was unusual for Jim to be so serious.

"In his room, sick." He looked back to her. Maybe he wanted to see her reaction.

Sheila began to turn pale. She looked at Jim then tried to gather herself. She brushed her hair back and inhaled. "He was all right this afternoon, except for a bad headache."

"When?"

"Right before lunch," she said.

"Did he eat anything?" Jim asked.

"First he wanted to go; then he decided to come home and have some rest," she said, very slowly, lowering her head.

"Did you two have any unpleasantness?" Jim asked, trying to get to the reason for Richard's headache.

"No. As a matter of fact, we had a very normal talk," she said, "but—"

"Yes, but what?" Jim looked at her impatiently. He knew there was something wrong, somewhere. "What made him sick?" He knew Richard was a very strong man. "Something must have brought him down."

Sheila didn't answer. She looked pale, confused, and worried. Jim looked for an answer in her face but decided that if there was anything wrong, they should work it out themselves. He knew Richard wouldn't be going anywhere for a couple of days, so he decided to ask Sheila to stay.

"Do you want to stay?" Jim asked coolly; maybe he felt a little sympathy for her, too.

"What's wrong with him? Will you tell me? Please. Why are you so worried?" she asked, her questions pouring out all at once.

"It's not just a headache," he said.

"Then what?" Sheila asked loudly.

He didn't want to worry her because he knew she was fragile. "I'm always worried, if anything happens to him or Sandra," Jim answered.

"I know that." She looked down. "But still, you see—I mean, I'm—you're making me worry, too. I'm human, after all." Her voice rose a little.

"Are you?" Jim's face was set; it was the first time she had ever seen him like that.

But Sheila was out of her mind right now. She knew something must have been very wrong with Richard. "What do you mean?" Her voice rose louder. "Please tell me, please!" Tears filled her eyes.

Jim thought for a moment, and then said, "Richard has some kind of tension on his mind. It could be dangerous, too."

"Oh God!" Sheila's face was red, tears were in her eyes, and she started breathing very fast. She always kept control of herself, but now she felt as if she were breaking up, as if something was happening inside her. She shook Jim. "No—say no. It can't be happening."

"Only if you help him," Jim said calmly. He was looking like a real doctor right now.

"Yes, I will. I'll help him. I'll stay here—until—until he's completely healthy and well, but…"

"Yes?" Jim looked at her.

"Will he be comfortable with me?" she asked impatiently.

"Yes, he will."

"I'm not sure about that," she said, still not believing him.

"I think so, and I'm a doctor, so if I say yes, then it's yes."

"All right, if you say so." She was still a little puzzled. Her heart was telling her to stay, but she was so confused that it was very hard to know what to do—so she took Jim's advice.

"Good." Jim looked relieved. "I have to go to the hospital. I'll ask Sandra to bring you whatever you need, and I'll be back later."

He grabbed his bag to leave then turned back. "Oh yes, I left medicine and a chart on his side table. Please give him his medication on time and write down everything that happens, even if he moves or says something, all right?"

She could only nod her head, feeling as though she weren't there.

For an entire week, Sheila didn't take a step outside the house. She didn't know what she was doing or why she was doing it. Only one thing was on her mind: Richard's health. His fever, his headache, and his quietness were her only concerns for now.

She slept on a sofa in Richard's room and followed all the instructions Jim had given her. Sandra brought some of her belongings. She came every day after school and spent some time watching over Richard, allowing Sheila to freshen up. Sandra gave Sheila her important schoolwork and made sure she finished it. In the beginning, Sheila couldn't study or even talk about school. But after a couple of days, Richard's fever went down. He smiled and recognized everyone, like normal. Jim was happy and relieved, and gave Sheila credit for Richard's improvement. Sheila couldn't believe it herself. She didn't know how she had been able to rise to the occasion.

"I think you should get some rest yourself," Jim said relieved, "because I don't need another patient."

Then Richard spoke up. "Sheila! Are you really sick? He knew that Jim was making fun of her." For the first time in a long time, Richard was smiling.

"No, I'm perfectly all right, Richard. You know, Jim was very worried about you; I think he should have some rest."

"Really," Richard turned his face towards Jim.

"I am fine, feeling excellent being boss in the whole hospital." He looked straight towards Richard proudly.

"I am glad for you, I think you both should have some rest" Richard said while he sat on his bed and pulled his pillow behind his back.

Sheila spoke again, and he didn't have enough time to take care of you and the hospital. So I promised him as a help to take care of you." She thought she could hide her feelings from everyone—maybe from herself, too.

Jim and Sandra saw each other and smiled and Richard closed his eyes and pulled his pillow back to lie down.

"All right," Sandra said, "now that he's getting well, it's time for you to get back to your regular life."

But Jim was thinking something else. He had watched Sheila all the time—how she had worried, how she had stayed awake most of the night. Sometimes he saw tears in her eyes, and once when he had come into the room, she had been praying.

"Right, Jim?" Sandra shook him.

"Oh yes, of course." Jim snapped back from his thoughts. "But I still need her help and she promised me, so I'm very hopeful that she'll keep her word, right, Sheila? You can take a rest, even start taking your classes, but at night, stay over here, please."

"Oh, of course, I will!" Sheila said and suddenly realized that Richard had turned his head and looked at her. Relief clearly showed on his face.

Sandra quickly looked to Richard and then to Jim.

"It's a promise," Jim said as he gave his hand to shake with a smile. Sheila put her hand into Jim's hand and smiled back.

Sheila helped Jim take care of Richard and his household. She actually enjoyed all the work. And she was able to go to classes and study. Richard was very happy these days and was recovering rapidly. Another week passed, and Sheila decided it was time to go back to her place. When she told Jim, he said, "Things look all right now." But Richard's face said something else—he did not want to let her go. And the same way Sheila's mind was also struggling.

Should I? Sheila asked herself. She knew the answer. But she was scared. She didn't want a marriage like her parents', but she didn't have the courage to leave Richard forever. She didn't have the courage to see other women with him, and she didn't have the courage to kill herself, either. She had to do things right. She had to have control of herself. That way she could have Richard, even if only as a good friend. That's all she wanted. All those things were coming in her mind at the same time.

"What are you thinking, Sheila?" Sandra asked.

"Oh, nothing. I'm just ready to go home now—I mean, to your place."

"I can see that," Sandra said.

"Yes, I am—why?" Sheila looked at her.

"May I ask you one thing?" Sandra asked seriously.

"Yes, of course, but what?"

I think she's nervous to go back, Sandra thought. "Did you talk to Richard? He looks worried, and this is not good for him, you can—"

"Worried for what? He's all right now." Sheila tried to control herself.

"I know, but he had a sickness of stress; you know that."

"I know, but I can't stay here anymore, I—I feel—"

"You don't have to stay, Sheila. I'm all right now," Richard said.

During his sickness, Richard had noticed Sheila's feelings about her involvement in the house, her management and control, how she had handled everything systematically, how much she had worried about him, how she had looked after him while he was sick, not eating, drinking, talking, or even opening his eyes. Sheila was always there, trying to feed him, making sure he drank enough water or juice, giving him all his medicine on time. In the beginning she had to give him medicine in the middle of the night. She had to set her alarm, sleep in the same room on the sofa, and get up every time he moved. This was why Richard was able to get well.

Sheila had given him hope and encouragement. He thought she might have feelings for him, or at least her fear was fading. He was happy to think he might be able to win her trust. So when he heard she wanted to go home, he went to her room to tell her she should go. He didn't want to pressure her into accepting him or living together. He felt strongly that a relationship worked only if both people wanted it to. He knew he loved her, but he wanted her to feel the same way about him. He couldn't force her to love him. That could come only from her.

Both girls saw him at once. He was standing in the middle of the doorway, with all his charms, except he looked a little bit pale. Sheila couldn't say anything. He said to Sandra, "You don't have to worry about me, see? I'm all right now, and I'm thinking of starting my regular schedule soon."

Sandra didn't know what to say; she just looked at him.

He came closer to her and put both his hands on her shoulders. Sandra looked at him but still didn't say anything. "I don't wish to have a sister. You know that," he said slowly, "because I have one."

"I feel the same way," Sandra said.

"OK, let's go and call Jim for my next week's schedule." He held her hands and walked toward the door, a stoic expression on his face. Then he stopped; Sheila was still looking at him. He turned and said, "Oh, Sheila, thanks very much for everything. You can go home. Get some rest and go back to school. I'll see you at work, day after tomorrow, all right? Bye." They walked out through the door.

With tears in her eyes, Sheila left. No one cared for her. How she had come to this house, she didn't know. She felt worse than she had the night she left her father's house. That time she had courage, anger, wishes, and hopes that her friend would help her. But now! She felt she had lost everyone, everything. Why? Why was she thinking like that? She missed school. All her friends were angry with her. After all she had done, this was her reward? *Oh, everybody is angry with me.* Richard, whom she had nursed back to health; Sandra, whom she always listened to; and Jim, who had asked her to help him. She tried to sleep, but she couldn't.

In the morning she was very tired, and her mind was exhausted; she felt weak. She got up, got ready to go to school, but couldn't go out the door. She went back to her bed. She stayed there for half the day, just thinking. And she thought, *let it go like that. Just stay quiet, try to do the regular things. Time will tell. Whatever is going to happen will happen.*

Around 1:30 p.m., she got up again, took a shower, ate a little, and had two cups of tea. As she ate, she remembered that Auntie, Sandra's mom, had come into her room a couple of times already. She went to Auntie's room to see how she was doing. Auntie was happy to see Sheila was back home and told her how much she had missed her. Sheila felt a little better; someone had missed her. "I'm very glad to hear that you missed me, Auntie. I wanted to come back, but Jim and Sandra needed my help."

Auntie said, "I know everything about that. How is he now?"

"He's fine," Sheila said then left the room.

She went outside to get some fresh air. No one had called her last night, and no one had come by to see her. Only Sandra's mom had checked in on her. Sheila thought for a moment that she should go to the hospital to see what was going on over there. What kind of changes had Jim made while Richard was not there? But she couldn't. She went back into the house, sat for a while outside of her room by the kitchen table and thought. Then she wrote some letters to other hospitals and offices right there through her cell phone. Around five o'clock, Sandra and Jim came back.

"Hello! Did you get enough rest?" Sandra asked her.

"Yes, I did," she said quickly, picking up her papers and going into her room.

"Do you want to go to work?" Jim asked loudly.

"Not today, Jim," she said, trying to keep her voice calm.

The next morning, she found Sandra waiting for her. "Let's go out I have time, so we can go together."

Sheila knew that Sandra was always very busy. Sandra stayed home only for things that were very important. Sheila and Sandra didn't say anything—they just walked together. Sheila realized that Sandra just wanted to get her out of the house so she could clear her mind. They had some conversation while they were walking. Sandra had to go to her job, before leaving she reminded her, "please go to work, they are waiting for you." Sheila had to go to work since she was working in this hospital. It was matching all her needs and she quit the first one and now she didn't want to get a different job—this was all she had but she didn't want to face Richard. After all she had done for him, he had treated her so rudely. But she needed to keep her job—for the money, the convenience, and the flexible schedule, at least for a while.

She started walking toward the hospital even though she didn't want to. Her brain was telling her to turn back, but her heart wouldn't accept that, so she kept walking.

5

"Dr. Jim Bradley, in the emergency room, please. Dr. Jim."

The announcement came from intercom. The voice was so different, or maybe Jim felt that way. He always ran in case of emergency. He ran into the emergency room as nurses and two doctors were trying to administer first aid. Jim went at the same time the nurse was announcing, *"Dr. Richard Beckman, in the emergency room please. Dr....."*

"Stop!" Jim shouted loudly. Please stop the announcement. "Dr. Richard just came back today after his long sickness. He's not able to do all this at once."

Actually, he didn't want Richard to see Sheila like this. He wanted to check her first and tell Richard a good excuse so he wouldn't get emotional. At the same time, Jim was examining her also, while thinking.

"Sheila!" Richard arrived. "What's happened? Jim, what's happened to her? Is she going to die? No, it can't be possible. God, don't give me that much punishment. Don't take her from me!"

"Calm down, will you? God knows how you became a doctor," Jim said as he pushed Richard into a chair.

More than an hour later, Jim found out Sheila had hurt the back of her head. She was unconscious right now, and he was pretty sure she was going to lose her eyesight or memory. He wrote on the chart and told a nurse to sit right there. He wanted to go on his rounds. He told Richard, "Let's go, we have to wait until she wakes up."

Richard just gave him an empty stare and smiled a little. "Do you know, Jim, who she is? This is Sheila—on this bed, unconscious," Richard said, pointing toward the bed. "I'm going to be right here, until she's well enough to be alone. I don't want anyone with her. I don't have to do anything. I mean—I mean, my mind is—"

"I know that," Jim interrupted him. "I'm going, and you just leave her like this." Then he tried to give him a shot.

"I'm fine," Richard said, as he took his hand away.

"What are you doing? I'm still your doctor, remember?" Jim asked. "I know what I'm doing."

Jim gave Richard the shot, just to keep him calm. Then he went on his rounds. Since Richard had become ill, Jim had become very busy. He had all the responsibility associated with the hospital. He wasn't spending enough time with Sandra; he wasn't home enough. But now! There was a completely different situation. For the first time in his life, Jim was very nervous, worried, alone, and helpless. He was sure Sheila was going to lose her eyesight. *Oh God, that poor girl! She had all those problems and now has to have this. I don't know for how long, maybe forever!*

No, I hope not. What's going to happen to Richard now? He just came back after his long illness, especially because of his tension, he was having headaches and fever. If something happens to Sheila, how could he even survive? Jim knew they both love each other very much. But Sheila's blindness of thought and blindness of judgment, or whatever it was that had caused this blindness Jim knew she loved Richard. During Richard's sickness, Jim had watched Sheila and had seen how much she worried about him. He had seen how much she did for Richard, day and night, tirelessly, without complain. She had taken care of Richard and his house. But why wouldn't Sheila admit she loved Richard? Jim decided that whatever happened to Sheila, he would talk to her about Richard. Jim was thinking like an older brother, and he wanted to help Sheila. He wanted to try to give her away to Richard like a brother. He trusted his friend. He knew him. He knew what kind of person he was.

Jim also knew that Richard loved Sheila and that even with all his charm, fame, wealth, and good character, he felt very alone.

Richard was always a quiet, kind, helpful, and hard-working man. He never got involved with any women. His friends used to ask him sometimes, "How come no girl ever impresses you?" He would simply smile.

"I'll know in my heart when I find the right woman," he would say.

Jim knew Richard was a man of honor, but now that he had fallen for someone, could he survive without her? Jim knew that Richard would have to try. *God help me. Give me courage, guide my efforts, and help my friend.*

The next morning, Jim looked at Sheila's chart, and as he had expected, Sheila had lost her eyesight. He took a deep breath and took a quick look at her. She was very quiet. *I think she knows already.* But Richard was very disturbed, pacing around the room continuously. *I think he's trying to take a big step. It was Jimmy's observation.* He looked sick himself. Sometimes he came and touched Sheila very lightly and sometimes checked the chart. He was not discussing anything about the treatment or whatever Jim was doing. Jim told the nurse to keep an eye on Richard, as well as Sheila, and make sure he didn't try to give her anything. Jim knew Richard was not in the right frame of mind to treat anyone, especially Sheila.

Within a day, Richard had regained control of himself. He went home, took a shower, shaved, and returned to the hospital. He also went to his office for a while then made his rounds to see everyone. He didn't prescribe any medicine or make any treatment decisions. Jim watched him closely, but also calmly and quietly. Two days later, Richard checked the test reports then talked to a few other doctors about her condition.

Each doctor had the same diagnosis and prognosis. Sheila had suffered a deep brain injury, she was unlikely to get her sight back, and she could be mentally disturbed. Richard was upset. He got up from his chair and started walking. Jim gave him a pill, and he took it quickly. He sat down again and closed his eyes. After a couple of minutes, he opened them back up.

"Dr. Jim Bradley," he said like a stranger, "if someone gives her one eye, can it be a successful operation?"

Jim looked at everyone and nodded his head. "Yes, but the sooner the better. And—"

"Get ready for the operation for one eye, Doctors." Richard got up from his chair.

"But how can I get an eye right away?" Jim got up, too.

"I have one," Richard was calm again.

"Where?"

"Here" Richard pointed to his own eye.

"Yours!" That was everyone's voice, except Jim's.

"Yes, I can work with one eye as well as she can."

"But maybe her vision will improve in the long run," some doctors said, trying to stop him.

"But I do not want to wait for the long run" Richard said. "Maybe it will be too late. Maybe she won't survive with this deep shock and maybe I'll lose control."

"I don't want to take a chance. I can't. Jim, you have to take my one eye so we both can live or take everything, because I'm going to lose my mind and destroy every thing anyway, so I won't be able to do anything." Richard picked up his file and left.

Jim begged Richard to change his mind and promised him he would find another eye, no matter how much money it would cost or even if he had to put an ad in the paper. But the answer was no.

Richard wanted to see her well as soon as possible. He wanted to sacrifice himself for her. Maybe he wanted to prove how much he loved her. Jim gave up and started preparations for a transplant operation because he knew that along with all his good qualities, Richard was a very stubborn man. Once he had decided something, it was final.

The night before the operation, Sheila asked Jim where he had obtained the eye. Jim first stayed quiet then told her very quietly, "Richard."

"What? Richard? What's happened to him now? Jim, tell me, please!" she cried as she got up from her bed.

Jim held her by the shoulders and tried to push her back. "Sheila, remember you always wanted a proof of love, trust, and a guarantee for being secure? You got everything, plus one eye, from Richard. He's donating you his one eye because he loves you so much that he doesn't want you to wait for another donor or just hope for your sight to come back."

"Oh my God! No, it can't be happening! I won't let him do that! No—no!" she screamed.

"Why not?" Richard screamed back at the same time. He had been listening to the whole conversation. He had come to see how she was doing when he heard Jim's voice. He was emotional and talking loudly. Richard wanted to hear and see the real happiness on Sheila's face. But he found out she was still mad at him; it meant she hated him so much that she wanted to stay blind instead of having an eye from him. And that's why he burst out, "Why not? I'm not hurting you; my eye will not bite you! You hate me that much that you can't even take my one eye? Just think of it as coming from a stranger!"

"Hate you? No, I don't hate—yes, I hate you, I hate you—very much!" she cried. "Please leave me alone. Let me go home; put me in handicapped camp. It will be better than that; I can't see you like that, please."

"And I can't see you like that, either," Richard said. "So please let me do whatever I have to do."

"I won't come back to you, so you don't have to worry about seeing me."

Richard was a little calmer now. "After your successful operation, I promise you, you will not see me again."

"But I don't want that!" she screamed again. "I—I, Richard, please!" She waved her hands toward him, and the next second she was in his arms, weeping. She held him so tight that her fingers were hurting him. Maybe she wanted to wipe away her mistakes, her being rude to him, her love that she had been hiding for so long, her misunderstanding about him and not trusting him. Maybe she was weeping because he did so much for her and she always had her pride, her demands that she had to have this and she couldn't do that, and he was accepting all her whims according to her needs and schedule. And now this sacrifice that he wanted to make for her, how could she repay him? Would he forgive her? All these questions were flooding her mind.

Richard was very emotional himself, with tears in his eyes. "I love you, Sheila, very much. Always, since I saw you for the first time, at first sight." He stopped then said it again slowly in a low tone so only she could hear him. He looked around the hospital room to make sure no one was listening. No one else was there—not even Jim. Richard continued talking in a low tone.

"I—I love you, too, always, but I don't think I'm good enough for you," Sheila said. "You deserve much better than me. Please forgive me." She was still crying as she held him tight.

He held her face up to him, even though she couldn't see him. She held him tight. Then his voice came in her ear very softly.

"Whatever I deserve, I got; whatever I am, I'm yours. All I need is your word, Sheila. Tell me you're mine—tell me, please." Richard lost control; he hugged her tight, straightened her hair, and wiped her tears.

"But—I—"

"No 'but.' You have to accept me; you have to say yes. We both love each other, so what else is there left to say?" He lifted her face with his hands. "Tell me, could you have a good life without me? Tell me the truth."

"No." She shook her head.

"Believe me, I can't live without you, Sheila. I can't."

She thought for a while then told him, "Only if you don't give me your eye. Promise, Richard, please." She shook him.

"You can't live like that."

"I can," Sheila said. "I can spend my life in blindness if I have you. After all, this is my fault. I misunderstood you,

I didn't trust you, and I didn't want to go back to work, but I had to—I was forcing myself. That's why all this happened. This is all my mistake, I should suffer—"

Richard stopped her. "Whatever happened, it's over," he said. "Now it's in the past. We should forget about that and think about the future."

"The future is that I should suffer." She stopped for couple of seconds—bent her head and inhaled. "I'll wait for a donor and pray for a successful operation."

Richard felt helpless but didn't say a word. He took a deep breath, pulled her closer to him, and said in a very low but strong voice, "Everything will be all right. Just be strong and never lose trust of me. I'm yours; we're together, no matter what happens. We'll face this together. OK, sweetheart?" He lifted her face up again.

She shook her head a little and let it rest against his chest. Then she said in a low but steady voice, "If you promise me that you will not give me your eye."

"It's a compromise," Richard asked.

"Yes," she said slowly.

He still held her tight.

"What are you thinking?" she asked.

"I want to keep my promise, but I'm not comfortable..." he said slowly.

"Being with me? I told you, there's no comparison between you and me." She tried to move away from him, but his hold became tighter.

He bent his face toward her head then said slowly, "I was talking about your eyes. I don't want to leave you in this condition."

"I'll be all right, until you can make some other arrangement."

"Are you sure?" he asked.

"Yes."

Jim had been standing guard outside the door so no one could disturb them. When Richard emerged with tears in his eyes and a smile on his face, Jim hugged him. "Now what are you crying for? Congratulations!" Jim said.

Richard said, "Thanks—for everything."

They looked at each other and patted each other's shoulders. Jim was relieved that Richard wouldn't be sacrificing his eye. "Don't worry, friend. We'll get one," he said.

"I hope so. The sooner, the better."

A week later, Jim told Sheila that she would be having an operation the next day. She had been so happy and relieved that she didn't bother to ask what kind of operation she was going to have, for one eye or both. She just said, "All right, I'm depending on you, brother, whatever you like."

The next day, she had her both eyes operated, and it was successful. Richard, Jim, and other doctors were there. Sandra came to visit her. As soon as she came out from her anesthesia, she called for Richard. He was there as always. She touched him to make sure he was really there, touched his eyes, then went back to sleep.

Doctors wanted her to sleep as much as possible. Richard stayed at her bedside, and Jim was doing more than enough for both of them. He was taking care of them as well as for the doctors and the hospital, on Richard's behalf. Sandra visited Sheila every day, talked to Richard, and helped Jim. She was working with him almost all the time.

The story of Richard and Sheila spread throughout the hospital. In every department everyone was talking about their love and offers of sacrifice to one another. Most were happy, while some were surprised to hear that Dr. Richard had fallen in love with a student. Most were happy for him, but some staff members didn't care. Others were just waiting to see what would happen next. Because Richard was so kind, humble, and hardworking, everyone knew him from all over the hospital, whether it was a doctor, nurse, office staff members, or security guard. If anyone needed help or wanted to talk to him, he would stop, listen, and try to assist. If he was in a hurry, he made sure he got back to the person. He was very popular, so his news was a topic of conversation for many people in the hospital. Everyone was working hard, especially Jim, who was handling Richard's responsibilities. When anyone asked about Richard, Jim would change the subject, saying, "Oh, I'm so busy these days that I don't know about my own wedding."

One day, Jim was in the emergency room and met with Dr. William. "Hello, Uncle. I didn't know you were here," he said and shook his hand. Then Jim looked at the bed where a woman was half sitting with the help of a pillow. "Who's she? Do you know her?"

Dr. William explained her condition to Jim in a few words and asked him to take care of her. He said he would keep in touch with him and come back very soon.

Days passed slowly for Richard but went by very quickly for Jim and Sandra –both were busy. This particular day was special for everyone, especially Sheila, who was very anxious, praying to God to give her eyesight back. Jim was worried, too, but excited. For Richard, every moment was important. He spent all his time with Sheila, waiting calmly for the time when Jim and the other doctors would remove the bandages.

Jim was on his rounds in the hospital, and Sandra was doing some paper work in Jim's office. Sheila was sitting in a chair; next to her hospital bed and gripping her chair handle tightly. Richard was trying to read the newspaper, but then he put it aside and started walking around the room. He looked at Sheila, took a deep breath, and then stood beside her chair.

"Sheila"—he touched her lightly on the shoulder—"how are you doing?"

Sheila touched his hand, then gripped it tightly and put her head on it. "You're still here!"

"Yes, of course. Where would I go?" He touched her hair with his other hand.

"Richard! What's going to happen? I mean—I mean if my eyesight doesn't come back. If—"

"Sheila," Richard interrupted, "you know that's impossible. We did the best we could do, and your operation was very successful." Richard tried to encourage her, but deep down he was very nervous himself, even with all his medical experience. Questions flooded his mind. But he held himself together because he didn't want Sheila to get more upset.

"Good morning. May I come in?" Jim was at the door with two other staff members. Sandra was behind Jim, and she was quiet and tired. "What's the matter with you two?" Jim tried to cheer them up a little, but everybody's face was set. Jim gave some important instructions to Sheila then started opening the bandages and cleaning her eyelids.

"OK, open your eyes very slowly," he told Sheila. He was right in front of her. Sandra was behind her, holding her by the shoulders. Two doctors were watching her, too. And Richard was standing a little farther away, very quiet, holding his chair tightly. Sheila held Sandra's hand very tightly; for a minute she missed her father badly, but the next minute she opened her eyes very slowly then closed them fast. Everyone jumped a little, and Richard sat in the chair. But soon she opened her eyes again slowly. *Jim… Sandra…docs…where's Richard?* She tried to turn her face, but Jim held her.

"Can you…" Jim asked with a shaky voice, "see?"

"Yes—yes, I can see." Her voice was a little shaky.

"Thank God!" everyone, including Sheila, said in unison.

She tried to turn her head, but Jim's hold on her was tight, so she couldn't move. He knew what she was looking for, so he ignored her and said, "Now close your eyes and open them again. Richard is right there." He turned her head very slowly to Richard's direction pointed with his other hand. "I know you can't recognize him; he looks like a clown."

At the same time, Sheila saw Richard—who was standing little away by his chair, very pale, unshaven, and wearing dirty clothes. "Rich—" she tried to call him, but Jim closed her eyes.

"Not too much light at once," he said. "All right, now you take some rest, and I'll tell this clown of yours to be himself again."

Everyone, especially Richard, was happy and relieved. But Sheila was disturbed, and she did not know why.

Why was she feeling something inside? Why was she missing her father so much? These days she was seeing her father in her dreams.

Every morning when she woke up, she wanted to see her father. Once the feeling was so strong that she went to the phone. She dialed the numbers for her father's home then hung up. She started walking and stopped in front of the mirror. She was afraid to see the new eyes. Why, she didn't know. "Oh God!"

These eyes are the same as Daddy's! For a second she thought, *No, it is not possible. He has his own life; he doesn't know about me.* Then the feeling came back. For a minute she thought *if he knew about me...maybe he feels sorry; maybe he wants to see me. If he wants to, I won't refuse to see him. I don't know how he is now. Maybe he has a new baby, a good life.* She was thinking and thinking.

"What are you thinking about? Come on; wake up from your dreams. I have good news for you," Sandra said, coming in the room fast.

"About what?" Sheila asked and looked at her.

"About your father—he's all right now, I think."

"Why, what happened to him?"

"Oh, I thought you knew already…"

"Knew what already? Is something wrong with him?" She jumped up and came close to Sandra.

"No, I don't know anything about him." She realized that Sheila wasn't supposed to know and that she shouldn't be put under any stress, which could affect her eyes.

"Then what are you saying?"

"Oh, I don't know what I was saying. I came to tell you we're getting married soon."

"What? When? So soon, I mean? You don't want to finish school? Congratulations, I'm so happy for you and Jim."

The next morning, Dr. Jim came to check on Sheila. After he checked her, she asked to see the man who had given her his eyes. Her conversation with Sandra the previous night had made her uncomfortable, and she wanted to meet or get a glimpse of her father.

"What's the connection with this?" Jim asked. "I mean, why do you want to see your father right now?" He was looking at her with a little surprise.

"I don't know myself," she said. "I want to see him so bad."

Jim stayed quiet for a while. "I don't think it is good for you to see him now."

"And may I ask why? I'm all right now."

"I know you're getting better, but you're still not completely well. I think you should wait a couple more days. Give yourself more time to be completely well. It is an eye trans-plant; it will take time to heal," Jim explained. "First you have to follow the instructions to save yourself from more compli-cations. We're checking everything. We'll let you know."

"But—I don't understand why it will be too much for me—why?" She was being stubborn and impatient "Sheila, I think the shock will be no good for your eyes or your brain," Jim said.

"All I want to know that who is he? Why did he donate his eyes to me? Is he ill or dying?"

"No—no nothing like that. He's getting well—very well."

"Then why did he donate his eyes to me?"

"Sheila, he did not *donate* his eyes to you; he *sacrificed* them."

"Who is he?" Sheila was getting emotional.

"Someone who loves you the most—more than any-body, and I promise you, if you will behave well, I'll let you see him next week."

Then she remembered Jim's marriage. She congratu-lated him and gave him a big hug.

She tried to ask the same question of Richard, too. But he didn't give her any satisfaction, except a promise to let her meet him sometime soon.

"Sweetheart, I'm a doctor; I know when you will be able to handle this new situation."

Sheila was very eager to meet this brave man. And she wanted to see her father, too. "I don't know why I want to see Daddy so much," she said.

"Because he's your father," Richard said.

"He's been my father since I was born, but now—"

"I understand that."

"Then…"

"You were ill, so natural feelings are making you want to see him."

"That is true, I guess." She was surprised herself; why did he keep coming into her mind? Whenever she looked at herself in the mirror, the urge to see him got stronger.

Richard talked to Jim about what he should do. "This is the time to tell her the truth and let them see each other," Jim told Richard.

"I think so, too, but I'm worried; she's very sensitive."

"Then talk to her first and explain everything. She's a sensitive girl, yes, but she's not naïve. And of course, she's a very brave and strong girl, too. You have to explain it to her. Tell her how much you love her and how much her father is doing for her and so on. This is the right time." Jim's voice was strong.

"I think you're right," Richard said, but he was still doubtful.

"Richard! What happened to you? What happened to your confidence?"

"Oh, it is nothing like that. I'm afraid—I don't want to go back again to those problems that I had before."

"It's not going to be like that. If you give me permission, I'll handle it." Jim looked straight into his eyes.

Richard looked back at him. He didn't say anything, but his eyes conveyed trust. He just shook Jim's hand and left the room.

The next morning, when Jim checked on Sheila, she was walking around the room, seemingly deep in thought, and looking uncomfortable.

"What's the matter, sis?" Jim asked.

"Good morning, brother," she said, looking at him with a little surprise.

He looked back at her, too, with a little smile.

"What?" she asked.

"You didn't give me an answer to my question."

"About what?"

"What are you thinking about?"

"Nothing, just thinking something." She bent her head.

"That can't be possible," he said, shaking his head.

"What can't be possible?" she asked.

"Nothing and something can't go together."

"Sorry, but that's the way I feel these days," she said and took a couple of steps here and there inside the room.

"It means you're feeling fine."

"Physically, yes," she said.

"About the mental problem, we know," he joked, and they both smiled. "Oh, you know?" Jim was testing her to see if Richard had told her who had sacrificed his eyes for her.

"What?" Sheila asked warily.

"Richard didn't tell you anything?" Jim asked.

"Yes, we had a little talk, that you will take me to the man who gave me his eyes," Sheila said.

"Yes, and you can see your father, too, if you want." Jim came one step closer.

"What's happened to him? Is he in the hospital?"

"Yes, he's a little bit sick, too," Jim, said slowly.

"Maybe that's the reason I feel this way these days?"

"Maybe," Jim answered while he read her chart.

"I don't know why. I want to meet him so badly. Whenever I see myself in the mirror, I feel—I feel he's seeing me. Watching my every step. I feel like he's with me all the time." She started walking around the room again. "I hope he's all right."

"Do you care? "Jim asked in a sharp tone.

"Well, he's my father, after all. That's all I have, Jim."

"And a brother." He looked at her seriously.

"I know you're an excellent brother. But—"

"And Richard," Jim interrupted her.

"You both are very important in my life. But—"

"But you don't believe in love and care about all these things?" Jim wanted to hear some more from her.

"I know now, after Richard's love, your care, and Sandra's care and help, I know how much I was wrong," she said, talking in a low voice.

"Someday you will realize about your father's love, too, sis; just wait."

"Maybe. Sometimes I feel like that, or maybe that is just my wish," she said, looking at him.

"Sometimes wishes come true." He looked at her, too. She did not answer; she just looked back at him. "All right, get ready for tomorrow."

"For what? Are you taking me to meet that brave man?"

"Yes!"

Jim left, and until the next day, Sheila felt disturbed and uncomfortable. She thought of different plans. How was she going to talk to him? How was she going to express her feelings to this courageous man? Her entire past came to the forefront of her mind like pictures, one after another. *Oh God! Maybe my father still loves me. Maybe he wanted to tell me the day that I fainted. Maybe his new wife left him and he wanted to tell me. I should listen to him.*

With all these thoughts, she passed the time. The next day, she was ready very early, before Jim was scheduled to come on his rounds in the hospital.

Richard came first. As soon as she saw him, she jumped up and ran into his arms.

"What's the matter? No hey or hello? Is something wrong?" Richard grabbed her tightly with one arm, and with the other hand, he touched her chin and raised her face.

"Richard!" She didn't give him an answer.

"Yes?" He was still holding her.

"Are you busy?" she asked.

"Yes, but may I know why you're asking?"

"Because—because Jim will be here any minute to take me to see the man, and my Daddy is sick, too."

"I see. Then go, if you're ready to see both of them at the same time."

"Yes, I am—but I wanted you to come with me, too. Will you, please?"

"I'm always with you, whether you want me or not."

"Thank you," was all she could say when she saw the love reflecting from his eyes.

Richard didn't give her an answer; he just held her tightly again.

Jim arrived. "Good morning, both of you!" He gave a salute.

"Hello, Jim. May I take Richard, too, please?"

"Yes, of course," Jim said.

"Let's go, then." She tried to walk out.

"One minute. Let me check your chart first," he said and turned to her bedside. Richard admired his punctuality and quickness. "Oh, one more thing, did you have your breakfast?" he asked.

"I'm not hungry right now, at all," she replied.

Richard said, "I haven't eaten anything myself this morning."

"Then you both should have your breakfast." Jim saw the food on Sheila's table and said, "I think this is enough for both of you. Or do you want me to order more?"

"That should be enough for us. I'm not hungry at all," Sheila said.

"I'll have just a little also," Richard said, pouring some coffee.

OK, you both finish eating. Then Sheila needs to take her medicine. He sat on Sheila's bed.

Richard knew what Jim was doing. He saw Sheila's medicine, which was intended to keep her calm, and he looked toward Jim. They winked at each other and kept quiet.

When they left the room, Sheila walked between Richard and Jim, nervous and confused. Once they got to the other floor, where Mr. Scoot was rapidly healing from his operation. Jim stopped at the door. "First I want you to meet that man, all right?"

Richard touched her shoulders. "Sheila! Are you ready for that?"

"Yes, of course," she told him quickly.

"All right, but remember one thing: I love you very much, and so does your father and—"

"And me, too," Jim said, pointing to himself.

"And real love is not supposed to be shown always, sweetheart. You can find that out, especially when you're in trouble. Sometimes, if someone is upset or angry, it doesn't mean that he or she doesn't love or care anymore."

She was looking at him; tears were in her eyes. "I'll remember, Richard. I will." Her voice was very slow and deep. Then they entered the room.

A man was sitting in the chair. He was skinny. His head was down, and he was wearing dark glasses, so Sheila had no idea who he was. Jim tapped her shoulder. "Go ahead."

The man looked like her father. She held Richard's hand and looked at him, feeling as though she didn't have any strength anymore.

Richard put one foot forward, and so did Sheila. After two steps, she forgot about Richard.

"Daddy—Daddy, it was you—you gave me your eyes! How could you do that? Why? Why?" she kept asking and crying. Her knees buckled and went closer to him. Her father was quiet, he held her tightly. His face, his heart, and his great sacrifice told Sheila every minute of his misery. No words were needed.

After a long time spent crying, she felt a little better. She raised her head and saw her father. He looked old and weak and was very quiet. "Daddy"—she put one hand on his shoulder—"I love you, Daddy. I've always missed you, but I thought—I thought you didn't need me anymore."

He didn't answer; his hold was just as tight as before.

She had a good talk with her father. She knew how wrong she had been, how much her father had always loved her, missed her, and cared about her. How lonely he had been since she left home. "Daddy, why did you do that?"

He kept his head down. It looked as if he was thinking of lots of different things. He looked as though he was tired of facing problems, tired of being alone.

"Daddy," she said again.

"Yes?" The voice came from far away, maybe from deep in his heart.

"Why did you give me your sight? No one stopped you from making that big decision, especially for both eyes?"

She remembered Richard's decision. "You could have given me one."

Her father answered, "No one could stop me, because I didn't let anyone do that."

"Why?"

"Because…" A long pause again.

"Because why, Daddy?" She wanted to hear everything from him. All that had happened to him after she left. She wanted to spend all the time with him, all the time she had lost. It was very hard to make him talk. He had always been a quiet man. She kept trying harder and harder, and after a long wait, he told her.

"After you left, I missed your mother more than before. Everything was looking different all of a sudden. In spite of my trying hard, I couldn't keep myself happy the same way as before. One day, I had a big argument with Samantha, and I called you. You collapsed; I knew something was wrong with you. I left right away to go to Sandra's house." He stopped for a minute. "Then I found out you were in the hospital. When I met with Richard and Jim, they were always very kind to me. They told me all about you and told me not to see you, at least for a while, because it was not good for your health. I came home, but I was more disturbed; all my attention was on you. A week later, I found out that you were all right, but my wife was so disappointed because of all my different attitudes and quietness. I neglected her and all those arguments made her sick so she couldn't take it. So she left me."

"Without informing you?" Sheila asked, surprised.

"She left a little note. And I never tried to get her back." He stopped for a while again.

"Why, Daddy? You wanted to start your life again. You were so happy and peaceful in those days," Sheila said.

"I know—I know, sweetheart. You know if someone loses everything, then gets even a little back, that person feels a lot, and that's what happened to me. I was happy, peaceful, and everything felt so right at that time, but that happiness was shallow. The day you left, my happiness left me, too. But it's come back now. I'm happy again; I've got you back, haven't I?" He held her by the shoulders.

"Yes, Daddy, yes—oh, I wish I knew all this before! May I ask you one more thing, Daddy?"

He nodded.

"Do you want her to come back? I mean, do you miss her? I can call her."

He paused then said in a very low voice, "We're finished. I didn't want to let her stay like that. She's a nice woman. It is me who lost three ladies in a row. Whatever you went through, it's all because of me. I had to give you your vision back; I want you to see this world with my eyes and your brain, and Anna's ideas. In a different way, with a bright vision." It felt as if he was talking to himself.

"All right, time to rest for the both of you," Jim said as he came into the room. Richard was waiting outside so they could have some privacy. Sheila's heart started to beat fast. She was thinking about going back home again. She remembered everything that had ever happened during those days. She went to her room and lay on the bed for quite a while but couldn't get to sleep. She got up and started pacing. She was very excited, worried, and sad about everything that had happened to her family, herself, and especially her father. *I hope it will never happen again. If I didn't listen to that woman's order, if I just didn't leave my father, or if I had a little control over my emotions and decisions, none of this would have ever happened.*

Now what should I do? I can't leave my father like that. "No, I can't," she said aloud. "This is my time to prove my feelings, my love, and my caretaking skills. I hope everything will be all right. I hope…"

"I hope so, too." Someone came into the room. It was Richard. "What are you doing up at this time? You're supposed to be in bed by now," he said.

"I know, but I can't sleep. But what are you doing here?"

"Checking on you, like always. How was that?"

"How was what?"

"Meeting with your father?" Richard searched her face for a clue to her true feelings.

Finally, she said slowly. "You knew all about it."

Of course we knew about it, he said proudly. Mostly Jimmy was taking care of that."

"Why—why not you?" She looked at him with a little anger.

"Because I was very upset myself," Richard said.

She looked at him for a couple of seconds then asked, "How are you feeling these days. I mean, any headache or any—"

"Nothing, I'm perfectly fine since I got you, all my tension headache, worries, everything is gone. I'm the happiest person right now."

"And I am, too. What's happening between the two of you?" Jim asked as he entered the room.

"Hey, what are you doing here at this hour?" Richard stood up with a look of surprise.

"To check up on both of you," Jim said. He was tired but relieved and smiling. "Leave my sister alone; she needs some rest now." He gave her a pill to take. "Good night, sis. Let's go now; we need rest, too." Jim walked out with Richard.

The next morning, they all went to Mr. Scott's room. Sheila and her father were both being discharged from the hospital. The difference was that one was blind, and the other was no longer blind. Now, she was healthy, happy, could see, and had her loved ones around her. Her father was old, weak, and needed a cane and dark glasses. But he had his daughter back, and he was ready to return home with mixed feelings.

"Well, are you ready to go home, Mr. Scott?" Richard asked as he shook hands with him. "You're a great man. You have a big heart. I'm very impressed. I promise you, as soon as I get a donor, I'll give you an operation. And you will see the world again."

"I don't want to see the world. All I want is to see you and my daughter happy and well again." Mr. Scott stood up with his cane. Sheila ran and held his hand. "Sheila"—he held her hand tightly—"after all these problems, I found these two men." He paused for a moment. "I don't want to force you into anything, but..." He stopped for a while again. "You can't find anyone better than him."

"I know, Daddy," she said slowly. Her eyes were down, her face turned red, and her heart started beating fast again.

Jim raised his thumb, and Richard gave a bright smile.

Sheila went home. Everything looked so different, disorganized. *Oh, this house needs help*, she thought. She went here and there and checked out the whole house. She noticed her father's room looked the same way as before. Surprise, Samantha had changed everything when she moved into the house, except Sheila's room. She remembered when her stepmother had come into her room and asked to move the furniture, but Sheila refused. Even Daddy didn't want to disturb her because he was aware of how she was feeling. So he said, "Everything is new for her, so just let it go for a while." She was thinking, *why did Daddy rearrange his room in the same way it was before?* Her heart ached. *He still misses Mommy.*

Oh boy—I forgot about Daddy. I'm not supposed to leave him like before. He needs help nowww, she continued thinking.

Oh boy—people are so ill-mannered here. Not offering a cup of tea, even, Jim said to himself. *All right, I'll get it myselfff*. Then he got up. At the same time, Richard came into the room after checking Mr. Scott's vital signs. He gave all the instructions to a nurse who was hired to stay with them for a while. Sheila got up to go to her father's room and see what he was doing.

"Where are you going?" Richard asked.

"To see Daddy," she said.

"I just came from there; he's fine, and besides that, Nurse Linda is there."

"Who's she?" Sheila asked, surprised.

"She's a nurse, and her name is Linda. She was hired to take care of Uncle while you weren't here," Richard said.

She sat down without saying a word. Richard started walking slowly toward her. She looked at him and said, "Thank you."

"You're welcome." They both looked at each other, lost momentarily in their own thoughts. Then Richard said, "Did Uncle Scott tell you his opinion about me?"

"Yes," she said, still looking at him.

"May I know yours?" he asked and bent down a little.

"Same," she said clearly.

She's so happy to come back to her home, Richard thought.

"Then may I?" He put his hand into his pocket and took out a little box, opened it, and took out a very beautiful ring. Then he looked at her; she was still looking at him. Richard raised his hand to hold hers. Her hand moved automatically and went to his hand. He put the ring on her finger. He held it awhile, and trying to bend his head to kiss her hand, before that she kept his hand on hers and stood up and put both arms around him.

"I am so happy to wear your ring," she said slowly." He agreed. She looked at him, while still holding him, "are you sure? I still do not believe that you chose me over all the other competitive girls."

He laughed and said, I have never been so sure in my life, sweetheart, we are lucky to have each other.

"Congratulations!" two voices said in unison.

Sheila and Richard looked at the door. Sandra and Jim were standing there and clapping with joy.

This looks like it was preplanned, Sheila thought for a minute.

"Thank you," Richard said. He looked very happy. So was she.

Sandra ran toward Sheila, hugged her, and gave her a kiss on the cheek, and then Jimmy kissed her on the other cheek.

"Let me show this to Daddy!" Sheila said and ran to her father's room. Richard followed her. Her father was sitting in the chair wearing his dark glasses, quiet.

"Daddy, would you give me permission for this?" She held his one hand and put it on hers so he could touch the ring.

"Of course, my darling, of course. I'm so glad to have both of you." He raised both arms to the two of them.

"My tea is getting cold. Let's come, everyone, please. It was Jim." Sheila walked between her father and Richard. She thought, *how lucky am I to have them both and* how blind was I to misunderstand both of them.

When she came to the dining room, the table was full of a variety of foods.

"Is this a party?" Sheila asked with surprise.

"Yes!" everyone said together, and Richard laughed for the first time in a long time.

Sheila was very busy after she returned home. She had to take care of her father most of the time. Richard told her not to come to work anymore. She looked at him with a little surprise, and he grabbed both her shoulders. They looked at each other for a while, and then she tried to move but he still did not let her go. He said slowly and politely, "Now, in my opinion, every thing we share equally. Marry me, and it will be official." He wanted to propose to her in his way.

She looked at him, laughed, inhaled, and looked at him again. "Believe me, I want to do the same thing, Doc, but I don't want to leave Daddy like this."

"I understand that. I don't want to marry too soon, but please don't make me wait too long—promise?" He wanted to make sure she wouldn't change her mind.

"Promise," she said brightly, and he let her go.

She was still taking classes. Sometimes she went to Richard, just to see him and help him a little if he needed it. One time when she was in his office, she saw that it was a mess.

Oh God, what's happened to Richard? I think he's doing a lot of work these days. She started fixing the room. Papers had been strewn about, and she was trying to put everything in its place. She had also brought some fresh flowers to put in a vase.

Richard rushed into the room, and then stopped. "Is this my office?" he asked, looking at Sheila with appreciation.

"Yes, you're in your same office," she said, smiling.

"Thank you, darling," Richard said.

"Well, what's happened to you? I mean, you look so exhausted," Sheila said.

"Yes, I know," he said, taking a deep breath. "I'm still looking for some papers."

"May I help you?" she asked in a soft voice.

"Why? Feeling sorry for me?" He turned halfway to see her.

"No, I just want to help you."

"Thank you. You did a lot." He picked up some paper. "I found it! I have to go," he said.

"Richard, take care of yourself."

"Well! I have to take care of other things, too. I can't take care of me alone," he said sarcastically.

Sheila didn't answer. She knew what he was talking about. She just looked at him and smiled a little. Richard wanted to get married as soon as possible. He had told her so many times that he couldn't stand being alone anymore.

She wanted to do the same thing, but she wanted to finish college first. And the main thing she wanted was her father's eye operation so he could start living by himself again. She always felt guilty. Despite what had happened in the past, one thing was always on her mind: *I'm not going to make another mistake and leave him in this situation. Never.* But Richard was having difficulty fulfilling his promise. Once he had even said he would put an ad in the paper to try to buy eyes for Sheila's father, but Sheila had stopped him.

"No, Richard, I think we should wait. You see I wasn't with him for a long time. I want to take care of him for a while. I want to be with him and in the house. I missed both for so long."

"I know that, but what about me? I'm missing you, too, every minute. Especially in the house when I'm alone, I need you," he said and put both hands on her shoulders.

"I know that, but please, give me some time."

Richard took his hands away. "You have all the time you need; I'm not rushing you. I'm just telling you about my feelings. I want you to be mine—all mine, as soon as possible."

"Richard! You're a very impatient person. I always thought that you were a very self-controlled and passionate man."

"I am, but not with you." He looked at her lovingly Sheila bent her head. "Why?"

"Why? Do you want me to tell you?" He smiled at her.

"Forget it," she said and blushed.

"But I want to tell you anyway."

"I don't want to listen," she said as she tried to turn away.

But Richard grabbed her. "You can't get away from me that easily."

"I don't mean that, OK. Tell me what?"

"Everyone has a double nature. One for everyone and another with—" He stopped purposely; she looked at him.

Their eyes met. "…And another with their partner in life." He looked straight into her eyes and pulled her to him.

Then the vibration of his phone interrupted them. He reached into his pocket and pulled it out. He answered it, and then talked to someone for a while. He looked worried again.

"Is something wrong?" she asked nervously.

"Yes. I have a patient; she hasn't had her memory for two years," Richard said, still holding her with one hand while talking on his cell phone.

Oh God. Did you find out why?"

"It is a long story; I don't know myself." He moved his hands around her shoulder slowly, put his phone into his pocked then both hands in his pockets and looked at her politely to listen to her.

"If you don't know, then how are you taking care of her?" she asked.

"She's actually Dr. William's patient. I'm just helping him. But—"

"But what?"

"I don't know. I just want to help her. She looks like a decent woman, a great lady, but with many problems. I want to know who she is so I can help her, but there's no clue to her identity."

"I see!" she said and looked at her watch. "I've been out almost two hours."

"Yes, you should go home; maybe Uncle Scott needs you."

"Do you need me—I mean, for anything?" she corrected herself.

Richard saw her and gave a smile, as usual. "I always need you—I mean, your help. But no, I'm fine; I have to go to a meeting anyway."

"See you later, then," she said and picked up her bag.

"C'mon, I'll drop you off on my way," Richard said as he held her hand.

She started walking with him towards the hospital-parking garage. Both sat inside the car and Richard started the car to drive, when Sheila spoke.

"Richard." She turned her face to him.

"Yes?" He was looking straight ahead.

"When you find out any information about that lady, will you—will you tell me, too, so I can help you help her?"

"Of course," he said as he stopped at the traffic light. "Remember, we promised to help each other." He looked at her face.

"I remember my promise," she said with a smile.

"Me too," he said and raised one hand as the car started running.

Sheila didn't find out anything about that lady for a long time. When she came home, her father was sick. She spent all her time taking care of him. Then it was time for Jim and Sandra's wedding. Sheila was very busy with Sandra because she didn't have anyone else. Sandra always used to tell her, "Sheila, I'm self-made. Be like me, act like me, and try to do the right things, and you'll be all right."

Now Sandra needed help, and Sheila filled that need. Sandra's mother welcomed the help. She was old, and her health was starting to fail. When she heard that her only daughter was getting married, she laughed and cried. Sandra told Sheila, "Mom is getting into a panic. I don't know what I should do for her. She wants to do this and that,"—Sandra waved her arms around in the air—"but she can't do everything."

"Then why did you choose your wedding date to be so soon?" Sheila asked.

"You can ask your brother the same question," Sandra replied.

"I can, but it must have been a mutual decision."

Sandra paused then said in a low tone, "He's being impossible. He wants me to finish my exams and that's it; everything else can wait. I had barely finished my exams, and I had to start planning for the wedding. My mother has so many health problems—"

"I'll help as much as I can," Sheila said.

"Who will you help? Me or Mom?" Sandra asked.

"Both," Sheila said.

"But you have your own problems with Uncle."

"Daddy will understand. He's very much in control now, and the nurse is there, so we can manage," Sheila said.

"All right, thanks," Sandra said with some relief.

"But I don't understand why Jimmy is being so stubborn," Sheila said slowly.

"He isn't like that," Sandra said.

"Then, what?" Sheila asked with a little frustration in her tone.

"He's worried about me, Sheila. He wanted to help me, which I did not expect."

"But he was helping you; you two always helped each other. He's always here, I know." Sheila talked fast without looking at her. Sandra started laughing.

"What's the matter? Why are you laughing? Am I wrong?" Sheila stopped talking and looked at her with a little surprise.

"Sheila, he loves me. He doesn't want to see me suffering like that: full-time job, going to school in the evening, then studying at night and on the weekends. It was too much for me as well as for him."

"How?" Sheila had calmed down now.

"Whenever he comes to see me, he has to help me study or help around the house. He wanted to help me financially, but I didn't accept that. You know he's a well-off, open-minded, carefree man. He wants to work hard but also live a good life. He told me that to help with my problems, he would either marry me or move in. So I had to give in."

Sheila stayed quiet for a while, and then said slowly, "I can understand his point of view, and he's a hardworking, responsible man."

The wedding was small but lovely; all of the couple's relatives, friends, and colleagues were there.

Sheila's father attended for a very short time along with his nurse and Jimmy's father. He didn't feel alone for a minute. Everything went very smoothly; then the couple was off on the honeymoon. Jim was very impressed with how Sheila had helped arrange the wedding.

"That's the way a person should respond when there are problems. I like the way you handled everything. Thanks, sis," he said to her.

"You're welcome, brother, but you're not going to forget me just because I'm handling things well?" Sheila asked.

"You're kidding," Jim and Sandra both said together. "We're a team, all four of us." Jim raised his hand in the air, and Sandra did the same, while Richard's hand was up already. Sheila raised her hand as well.

"While we're away, will you do me a favor?" Sandra asked with a look of slight concern.

"Sure, tell me," Sheila said.

"Could you keep an eye on my home and my mother, please?"

"Of course—once it was like my home, too," Sheila said.

Richard chimed in, "Just go on your honeymoon without worrying; everything will be fine. We're here; don't think about anything—"

"Except for the both of you," Sheila completed the sentence and looked at Richard, who was looking at her and smiling.

"As soon as we come back, she won't be your responsibility," Jim said.

"We know that," Richard and Sheila said together.

While Sandra and Jim were on their honeymoon, Richard found an eye donor, and Sheila's father had to have the operation right away. Sheila was very worried. *God, help me, help Daddy, and help Richard, who's doing all this.* She stayed by her father's side because Jim and Sandra weren't there. Richard was extremely busy. He was taking care of Daddy as well as that new patient and was in charge of the whole hospital. He had to take care of other things, too.

Sheila was trying to help him as much as she could. But most of the time, she was with her father, taking care of him. Richard said, "This is a great help for you to take care of Uncle Scott." Sheila was so busy and worried about her father's vision that she never thought of anything else.

The day before Mr. Scott was to have his bandages taken off, Jim and Sandra returned from their honeymoon. The next morning Richard called Jim back to remove the bandages. The operation had been successful! Richard was able to come by right before Jim started opening the bandages. Sheila ran to him and held him tight. Richard was very quiet, even though he had full confidence in the success of the operation.

The bandages came off, and Mr. Scott opened his eyes—slowly—closed them back, and opened them again. Right in front of him, his eyes were looking at him and shining in Sheila's face. Richard was standing there, too, worried and anguished. Mr. Scott smiled a little, and then raised both arms towards his daughter, and she ran to him.

"Oh, Daddy! Thank God, you can see now! I'm so happy for you!" She laughed with tears welling in her eyes. Mr. Scott smiled a little, and then he raised his other hand for Richard, who was right there. He looked very happy; then he shook hands with Jim and hugged him.

"Thank you, both. I always wanted to have a son, and now I have two," he said, looking at both of them.

"My pleasure, sir," Jim said.

Mr. Scott looked at him. "I'm your uncle, and you know that."

"Yes, I know," he said as he bent his head.

Other doctors and nurses were there, too. He said thank you to everyone. Jim did not let him to talk much. He covered his eyes and let him take rest.

6

The lady was still in the hospital. She was getting along very well but kept very quiet, just observing everything. All the doctors' opinions were the same; she was thinking about something or trying to find out something because sometimes she looked very disturbed and contemplative. And Richard was very disturbed, too. One morning he came to her room on his usual rounds. That lady was sitting in the chair with her eyes closed. She was rubbing her hands slowly together. Richard found out she was awake and thinking.

"Good morning," he said loudly.

"Good morning, Doctor." She opened her eyes.

"How are you?" Richard tried to be very bright.

"I think I'm all right, Doctor…"

"My name is Richard Beckman; but you can call me Richard," he said.

"Richard, calling you by name is being friendly," the lady said as she looked at him.

"Yes, that's right; I want to be your friend," Richard said quickly.

"Why?"

"Something is in you. You look like someone very special to me."

"I know! Sometimes I feel it, too, but maybe because I don't have anyone." She looked disturbed and uncomfortable again.

"Me either," Richard said.

"God forbid, don't say that!" the lady said.

"Well, that is the truth," Richard said.

"Really?" The lady asked so normally that Richard forgot for a minute she did not have any memory or had some kind of sickness.

"Do you want to hear my story?" he asked in an even tone.

"I'd love to," she said.

"Well, when I was a baby, my mother died. My father took care of me all by himself; he was my mother and father both. And three years ago, he died, too. "And now this hospital and all of you are my friends."

The lady was looking at him very quietly.

"I want to help you, if you can tell me anything you remember."

She shook her head. "No, I only know Dr. William and his wife." She stayed quiet for a while.

"Dr. William, you know him?" Richard asked with a little hope.

"Yes, I was living with them. But why are you asking?"

"Oh, I met him one time."

"Because you both are doctors?" she asked.

"Yes, I think so" he said.

"Good to hear, that," she said with a smile and looked very normal. No one can figure out that she is sick. And if she is sick what type of sickness does she have? Richard was quiet. He wanted to let her think.

"Why not find yourself some girl for your life?" she asked.

"Oh, I'm engaged," he said with a smile. "Would you like to see a picture of her?" He put one hand to his inner jacket pocket and took out a little picture of Sheila. "Here she is," he said as he raised his hand to show her.

"Thank you," she said and took the picture.

"She's beautiful. I think I know her; yes, I do know her. Where? She looks like me—I'm feeling so close to her. Why? Why? Richard, Doctor, why?" She was disturbed again, very much.

Richard sat down on the edge of the bed, close to her chair. "Think, where did you see her? Her name is Sheila."

"Sheila…Sheila…Sheila what?" she asked impatiently. "Sheila what, Richard?" She was calling his name in a very disturbing tone.

"Sheila Scott," Richard said very slowly.

"Sheila Scott," she repeated the same way. Then tears came to her eyes, and she began weeping wildly for a long time. Richard didn't try to stop her; after a long time, he gave her an injection and asked her to take a rest.

He thought, *maybe rest will clear her mind and she can remember her past.*

"Will you leave this picture with me for a while, Doctor?" She forgot to call him by his name again, as he had requested.

"Sure," he said, "and I'll show you some more pictures soon. But right now, you just get some rest." He helped her lie on the bed.

"That's what you want me to do?" she asked, like a baby.

"Yes, it is very important," he said.

She closed her eyes. Richard watched her for a while to make sure she was sleeping.

The next morning, he collected more pictures from here and there and made an album. When he came to her room, she was sitting on the bed; the picture was still in her hand, and she was looking at it. She was so quiet and absorbed that she didn't notice when Richard arrived. He watched her for a while then put the album to the side.

"Good morning!" he said brightly.

"Good morning," she said as she looked up at him.

"How are you feeling?" he asked, hoping maybe she remembered something from her past.

"I'm all right, thank you." She gave him a glance then bent her head down and started looking at the picture again.

"Well, do you remember anything now?"

"No, not at all, but I wish I remembered. Oh, something is not coming to my mind." She shook her head.

"Well, maybe this will help you." Richard gave her the album. He sat right beside her and very slowly started turning the pages. Many different pictures were there, from when Sheila was a baby up to now. Mr. and Mrs. Scott were young, and they had many different types of occasions like birthdays, picnics, and some get together. Richard was explaining, too.

The lady was stopping all the time, looking very disturbed. And then she said, "When we went to that party. Oh, it was a very good one."

Richard jumped. "Do you remember?"

"Yes, but with whom, I don't know."

"Try to remember." Richard touched her one shoulder lightly. "And you will; I know that," he said encouragingly.

She began to look more disturbed. "All right, I'm tired now. I want to take a rest." She was out of thoughts again.

He put the pictures aside, checked her quickly, and gave her a pill to make her sleep. Richard was very much disturbed. He was thinking: *what should I do to make her remember her past?* He didn't want to tell anyone because he wanted to make sure himself, first. Who is she? He wanted to make sure of everything about her, but it was getting impossible. She often looked more disturbed and weak, and it was bad for her health, too. He sat thinking; his eyes closed and his head resting on the back of the chair.

"Now what's the problem?" Jim asked as he came into the room.

"Good morning," Richard said.

"Good morning. I asked, what's the problem now?"

"I always have some problem; you know that." Richard replied.

"I see," Jim said, looking at him.

"I'm in a hurry right now. I'll see you this evening," Richard said as he got up. "But I have to—"

"Avoid me," Jim interrupted. "That's all right. I'll see you tonight at your home," he said, and he waved his finger at him.

"All right, all right, we'll have dinner at seven. Just you and me."

"All right," Jim said.

Richard lifted his head to see him smiling, and Jim raised his thumb. Richard gave up finally, like always, and said, "You know that lady who is Dr. William's patient?"

"Yes, I know her. I told you about her the first time. Actually, I should call Dr. William about her latest condition," Jimmy said.

"Yes, of course. You can inform him, but the latest situation is completely different."

"Latest condition is what? I just saw her this morning. Is something new?"

"Yes," Richard said, "everything."

Jim heard the whole story; he looked worried for a while, too. He stayed quiet, thinking. "I think you should talk about this with Dr. William and find out about her past," Jim said.

"I did already," Richard replied without looking at him.

"If it's possible, you tell me, too," Jim said slowly.

"Yes, of course," he said. "Everything about her, whatever I hear from Dr. William."

"It means this accident happened at the same time."

"Yes," Richard said slowly.

"How can that be possible?" Jim asked.

"I'm thinking the same thing." Richard's head was still down.

"Wait a minute; this Dr. William is the same one who was involved in Sheila's accident, too?"

"Unfortunately, yes; he was there at that time, too. I think he mentioned that as well."

"Mentioned what?" Jim asked.

"That two years ago he almost had the same problem."

"Did you ask Sheila when her mother had died?" Jim asked. He just forgot that he was there—with Sheila—in the house when his father was running around with Uncle Scott and the lawyer.

"It was the same day," Richard said slowly, "but they identified the body, and the pocketbook was hers, too," Richard explained to him.

"That's right," Jim said, and tried to stand up. He always does that. Whenever he's worried or disturbed, he starts walking. Richard knew his nature. He stopped him.

"Sit down. This is a restaurant!" Richard's head was up.

But Jimmy didn't hear that, sat straight and kept holding the chair handles. "I think"—he raised one hand—"I still think you should tell Sheila, and ask for her help."

"I'm thinking that, too. Maybe the lady has a daughter like her or something." Both got up, too.

7

Dr. William was a neurologist and was very educated and experienced in his field. He always wanted to explore and do research to gain knowledge so he could help others. Occasionally, he gave lectures and attended conferences and seminars. Other hospitals asked his advice, and sometimes he was invited for his expertise.

He had two grown-up children, settled, and his wife usually went with him wherever he went on his special appointments. She liked to do research and help people very much; she enjoyed her trips as well.

This time, as usual, he came to another state for a seminar; he finished his meeting and was going back to his hotel. All of a sudden, traffic started slowing down. Police cars and ambulances were approaching. He felt it was his obligation to look; maybe they needed his help. He stopped his car on the side of the road and got out, walking around the corner to see what he could find out. He learned that a woman had been hit by a car and died.

"Sorry to hear that, are you sure that she is dead?" he asked.

"And another is injured on her head," someone said.

"Where?" He looked in the direction the man was pointing, halfway between two streets. Dr. William started walking fast in that direction; others were following him, too.

Someone said, "Maybe he's a doctor."

"Yes, I am," Dr. William, replied.

He saw a woman trying to sit; she was holding the fire hydrant and bleeding badly. Dr. William didn't know what came over him; he just lifted her, covered her head with a thick towel, and let her sit in his car. "I'm taking you to the hospital, OK, ma'am?" he said while he was driving. For a minute he thought he should inform the police first, get some information. But no, by the time he went through all the procedure, she would bleed to death like the other woman. He called the police from the car while driving, gave his name and ID number, told them which hospital he was taking her to, and even gave his license-plate number so they could locate him easily. He was well known at the hospital, so he had no problem admitting the woman quickly.

Dr. William and the hospital staff worked hard to save the woman's life. When he finally returned to his hotel, he told his wife everything. She was a very sympathetic woman and asked if she could help him in any way. A couple of days passed. The woman was getting better. The wound was bad but not very deep; it was healing fast. But there was a problem. She was very quiet and unable to give any information about herself, about her family, or about anything.

Dr. William diagnosed her memory loss but could not tell if it was permanent or short-term. She appeared to be alone. No one came to look for her; no one called. No one responded to reports on the radio and television or in the newspaper. Nobody could find any clue as to what her identity was. The hospital couldn't keep a patient indefinitely, especially without payment.

Although Dr. William was a little concerned about the hospital bill, he was mostly worried about the patient. When she recovered from her physical injuries, where would she go without her memory? She looked like a decent and educated woman. He was pretty sure she came from a good family. It was hard to just leave her. *No, I'm not going to do that.*

Dr. William wanted to advertise with a picture so someone would recognize her and come see her. But Mrs. William objected. She wanted to wait until the woman's memory came back so she would know what she had been doing and where she had been going.

Dr. William said, "I can't leave her like that, and we can't stay with her for so long."

"Then what should we do?" his wife asked.

"Think of something before it is too late."

"I have a solution," Mrs. William said.

"What is it?" He was curious as she often gave him good advice.

"Take her home. That will be the best thing to do," his wife said brightly.

"Will you take care of her?" Dr. William raised his eyebrow and looked at her.

"We'll take care of her," Mrs. William replied. "After all, she's not sick; she just lost her memory because she hurt her head and lost so much blood. She's still very weak."

Dr. William smiled a little. "She has a very deep wound that could be dangerous, too."

"But it is healing. I spoke with her; she talks normally, understands and replies perfectly well, and I have a feeling that she's an educated woman. It is sad that she does not know who she is. And she will go elsewhere and lose her identity."

"And being with you, she will not lose her identity?" he asked.

"Of course not." She looked at him. "You're smiling; are you trying to make me feel like a fool or just judging my interest?"

"Both," he said.

"And you made a decision already?" Mrs. William came closer to him.

Dr. William laughed. "What do you want?" He knew his wife was a very softhearted and generous woman. She worked in his hospital just so she could help people. She did research so she could be more useful, and she spent all her extra time helping others. That's what she was trying to do here. She did not want to leave the woman alone until she got her memory back or someone claimed her, without publicizing her situation so no one could take advantage. It was risky to take responsibility for someone else, especially someone they didn't know—someone who didn't even know her own name.

As a brain specialist, Dr. William met with many patients and knew they all had very different problems. He tried to treat them, help them, and listen to their problems. Sometimes he had to collect information about a patient from others because as a neurosurgeon and a psychiatrist, he realized quickly whether a patient was telling him the truth. Patients with mental conditions sometimes did not know what they were talking about. Sometimes they tried to manipulate the doctors. In those cases, doctors had to make their own decisions and treat patients according to established protocols.

With this patient, Dr. William had a very different feeling. She had lost her memory completely. At the same time, another woman had died. According to the police report, the dead woman had a family. *So who is she? Where did she come from? Is there any connection between them? Did she have any involvement with any crime?* After all, it was dark She was alone, not carrying anything, money or pocketbook. Maybe she had come out for a walk. Could be possible; weather was perfect that night. But why was she alone at that time? Maybe she was alone, maybe she was disturbed, or maybe she was living in that area and came out earlier for a walk after work, went home, and realized she had lost something. Could be her house key, jewelry, or some important paper; could be anything she came out to look for and because of that sudden accident, she was looking toward the other side of the street, bumped into a fire hydrant, and hurt herself. *Yes, that must be happened. Mrs. William is right; I can't leave this woman alone, without memory, without money, and without her own place to call home. I'll talk to the administrator of the hospital tomorrow*, he decided.

Dr. William wanted to check everything, but he did not have much time. He had to go back to his hospital. He got all the basic information from the police. Then he talked to the hospital's administrators and took responsibility for the woman's hospital bills. He was taking a chance, but it was what his wife wanted, and he felt it was the right thing to do. He accepted all legal responsibility for the woman, for as long as she had memory loss.

On the last day before they took the lady from the hospital, Dr. and Mrs. William went to her room. She was lying down on the bed with her eyes closed. He read her morning report. Mrs. William read her report with him, too. Usually doctors don't let anyone read a patient's chart without the patient's permission. But in this special case, he was handling everything in a completely different way. Maybe this was different. He wanted to help the woman. He wanted to know where she belonged and why no one had come to help her or visit her. After all, if she lived here, someone should know her. She must have had some friends or relatives. It seemed as if he and his wife were the only people who cared about this woman, so perhaps that was why he let his wife read her medical chart. After checking everything, he went to talk to the patient. She was sitting halfway on the bed with a pillow behind her.

"How are you feeling?"

"Very good, Doctor," she answered very politely.

"Do you remember your name?" he asked.

"No." She shook her head.

"Anna," Mrs. William said.

"Anna," the lady repeated, looking at her.

"While you don't remember your name, we'll call you Anna, if it is OK with you," Dr. William said.

"I don't have any choice? Thanks," she said with tears.

Mrs. William held her shoulders. "Don't cry. We'll be fine, live like a family."

"Who are 'we'?" Anna asked, looking at her.

"Oh, we're going home." Mrs. William held her hands.

"Where am I going?"

"With us," Mrs. William said.

"Is that all right with you?" she asked Dr. William.

"Oh, it will be a pleasure, if it is all right with you," Dr. William said.

"I'll appreciate that," she said in a very polite tone.

"Only we live in the house, and most of the time, I'm out, so you both can keep each other company."

"But how long will we go on like that?" Anna asked.

"As soon as you have your memory back, I promise, we'll take you wherever you belong."

"Thank you very much," she said and got up from the bed.

That was how she came to live with them. They were a very nice, decent, and educated family. She never felt alone. Dr. and Mrs. William had two children, a son and a daughter; both were married and had their own families. Anna had a chance to meet both of them.

She tried to keep herself busy, but her missing past was always on her mind. She was determined to find out about her past. *Who am I? Where do I come from? Why did I have an accident?* And the most depressing thought was, *No one ever came to look for me. Maybe I'm alone.* She shivered at the idea. Curiosity, aggravation, and depression made her weak. Sometimes she laughed and was happy and very active, but mostly she was down and trying to push herself back up. Dr. and Mrs. William watched her closely. Sometimes he tested her, and then Dr. William would prescribe a different medicine. Which he gave to his wife for her to administer. "Try this. Maybe this one will help."

And in that way life was passing, mostly good, as long as she didn't think about herself. But whenever she was alone, she couldn't think about anything else. Who was she? Where did she come from? She was certain of one thing: *I'm from that state where I had the accident. I should go back there, go to the same place where I had my accident, walk around, talk with people; maybe I can gather some information. Maybe I can collect some clues from here and there and my memory will start working again.*

One day she mentioned that to Dr. and Mrs. William. "If I go back to that place again, maybe I can remember something."

"Which place? Mrs. William asked."

"Where I had this accident, she said slowly."

Dr. William agreed with her and said, "My next assignment is there very soon; I was thinking that we would take you with us."

"Really?" Anna was surprised to hear that. "I think finally God is listening to my prayers," she said slowly.

"Maybe, but prayer alone does not help," Dr. William said.

"I know."

"You have to help yourself," Mrs. William said with a smile.

Anna looked toward them. "What should I do?"

"Are you taking your medicine regularly?" Dr. William asked.

"Yes."

"Then just rest, relax, and don't think too much. When you get there, try to observe everything." Dr. William got up. "And one more thing"—he looked at his wife—"this is a very short assignment. So please, you don't have to visit the hospital. Keep her company. Take her places, especially where she had that accident." All three looked at one another. Mrs. William looked at her husband and smiled because she knew what he was telling her.

" When are we leaving?" Anna asked.

"Next week. I don't know exactly. Good night." And they went to their rooms to go to sleep.

It was very hard for Anna to be patient. She was waiting for Dr. William to tell her when they would leave and how long they would stay there. She knew that Mrs. William would be with her to help and research with her from place to place. *Maybe I'll get my memory back…maybe*, she thought.

Finally the day came when the three of them flew to same state. Everyone had different feelings and thoughts.

It was a routine for Dr. William; he always accepted offers wherever he was needed. Sometimes urgent, other times by appointment, like this one.

Mrs. William was very excited. Most of the time she was with her husband, helping him and making notes.

Anna had a very different feeling. She was excited, hopeful, and ambitious. She was praying silently because her whole life was dependent on this journey. *Dr. William will not take me again and again. During my stay at his house, he traveled alone for so many times. They never complained.* Once Mrs. William mentioned casually, "I always used to go with him for company."

"I'm sorry; because of me you're staying," Anna said.

"No, not at all. I mean, now I have my company here, with you," she said and touched her shoulder.

"Thank you, but I can stay alone for a couple of days; it should not be a problem."

Mrs. William looked at her, smiled, and stayed quiet.

That's the way the days were passing. And now, Anna was traveling with them, for the first time, *and hopefully the last time*. She prayed again.

When she landed at the same place where she thought she had lived all her life, she did not recognize it at all. She looked toward Mrs. William, who looked at her and understood her problem.

"Don't worry at all; we'll go places together." Anna was very thankful for her.

The first day they were traveling, an accident happened: someone ran out in front of a car. She became very emotional.

She didn't remember anything after that. Maybe she got sick again. She was admitted to the nearest hospital, and Dr. William asked Jim to keep her under his observation.

8

Sheila was very quiet and uncomfortable these days. *Maybe because I'm alone*, she thought. Sandra was busy with her new home and new married life. She was excited because she was going to have a baby soon. Her father was very busy with starting his life all over again, which was disorganized after her mother's death.

She was sick because of that accident; during her sickness she found Richard's love and her father's sacrifice. Because of all those things, a couple of months passed very fast.

Then her father's eye operation, Jimmy and Sandra's marriage, all those big events made her very busy, and time flew. But now situation was different.

Jimmy was like a brother to her. Whenever they saw each other, he tapped her on the shoulder and after sometime asked how she had been. She understood.

There was no complaining. She was very busy, too, with her father's health. After a long time, she had her home back again. Her father was all right now. His behavior was excellent with her. She wanted to finish school because she knew Richard wanted to marry her as soon as possible.

She used to spend all her extra time after school with Richard. They'd eat together most of the time; when he was busy, she'd stay in his office. If he wanted her help or wanted to discuss something, they would talk about almost everything. But now! Almost a month, he looked different, very busy. In the office he always started reading books, looked disturbed, and tried to find solution for some problem.

At first Sheila thought he had some complications with some patients, and she tried to talk about that. But when she didn't get a good answer, she felt hurt. *Richard promised to tell me everything, but he's hiding something.* The next day she got up early and went to the hospital. *I'll find out.*

As soon as Richard came into the office, she was already there. She looked at him. As usual, he was tired, and his eyebrows were up. He came in and started looking for something, and she walked slowly toward him.

"Richard," she said, touching his shoulders with her hands.

"Yes?" he said, still looking away from her.

All of a sudden, she didn't want to talk about it anymore and changed the subject.

"Do you want to eat something?"

"No, not now, sweetheart," he said in a low tone and started looking for something again.

"But I'm hungry."

"Have something." He turned to face her. His voice was soft.

"Not alone," she said.

Richard stayed quiet for a while, and then smiled a little. "All right, go and fix something. I'll be right there." He put one hand on her shoulder and pushed a little. She made two cups of coffee and two sandwiches, put some fruit on the table, and waited for him. She tried to figure out how to start the conversation. Richard was a very gentle, calm, quiet, and busy man. But still something in him was different from any other man. When he was serious, it was hard to speak to him about anything. Even Jim had difficulty finding out anything from him.

Sheila was thinking about this when Richard came and sat in front of her; a file was in his hand. He was reading. He looked at her and started eating.

Sheila didn't touch anything; she just looked at him.

"What's the matter?" Richard asked with surprise.

"Nothing," she said slowly.

"You said you were hungry?"

"Yes, I'll eat. May I asked some—"

"Sure, sweetheart, you can ask anything. You know that." He bent his head to read the paper again.

She didn't say anything.

"Yes?" He looked at her with his eyebrow up and had a bite. "What's your question?"

"You—you look different these days. Do you mind if I ask you why?" Her voice was very slow.

Richard put his file aside and sat straight in the chair. "I look different? In what way?" Now he was looking straight at her with his usual little smile.

"Every way. You look worried, exhausted, busier than ever, and I want to know why."

"Because of my work. You know that I missed a lot; besides that, I'm a doctor. I have some responsibilities, too, and that's all."

"Yes, I see."

"Come on. Eat something so I can go," he said and smiled a little.

But Sheila shook her head. "I'm not hungry."

Richard put his sandwich down and bent a little. "Do you want me to feed you?" he said mockingly.

Sheila got angry. "No, thank you! I want to go home now." She started picking up her things.

Richard remembered that day when she left angrily from his home after his recovery from the long illness. *That is not going to happen again*, he said to himself and held her tight. "No, you're not going anywhere."

"Why not?" she asked.

"Because I don't want you to," he said, looking at her.

"Richard, let me go home. I want to go," she said again.

"Not until you give me a reason."

She looked at him but didn't say anything. Richard made her sit again, and he sat beside her. "Now tell me. What's the matter?"

"What's the matter?" She looked at him eye to eye. Her face was red with anger.

"Why are you angry with me?" Richard's voice was very calm.

"Because—because you promised me, not to hide anything, but you are; you don't let me do anything. You won't let me help you. I want to help you. You don't even give me any answers. You're always busy, always thinking about something. I want to know what the problem is," she blurted out.

Richard was still smiling. "You look good, very beautiful; I think I should do that more often."

"What?"

"Make you angry," he said, raising his hands to take the file. But Sheila grabbed it first.

"May I see this file?"

"No," he said and took the file from her hand.

"Why?"

"Why do you want to see it?" He was serious now.

"So maybe I can help you in some way."

"There's nothing in here that you can help me with, Sheila. If I need help, I'll let you know." He got up and looked at his watch. "I'm late already. You finish your lunch, all right?" He touched her cheek and left the room.

Tears came automatically. She was crying when Jim opened the door and came into the room. He stopped suddenly. "What's happened?" He was in a hurry, too, but he came to her. "Well, I'm alive. Why are you crying for?" He sat beside her.

"Well, good to know that."

"Just checking." He laughed at her. "Must be some-thing big, huh?"

She started crying more.

"Stop that!" Jimmy said loudly. "And tell me, what's the problem now?"

She told him what she was thinking, in short words, and said she was going home.

"I will, too, if you just wait fifteen minutes," Jim said as he got up. "Finish your lunch."

"I don't want to eat," she said.

"OK, then I'll help you finish it." He picked up the sandwich and broke it in half. "All right, we'll have half and half." He started eating. "Whose coffee is this?" he asked.

"You can have it," she said.

"And whose coffee is this? I think its Richard's. I know he was in a hurry, so he had half a cup and left. That's OK; you can have his, and I'm drinking this full cup and eating half a sandwich. Please finish your half because five min-utes have passed and I have only ten minutes left."

He spoke so fast that Sheila stopped crying and said, "That's all right; I'll go by myself." She started picking up her bag and books.

"No, you're not going anywhere by yourself." He, like Richard, remembered the previous incident.

"Why not?" Sheila asked, surprised.

"Because I have to go, too, and you know I always like company."

"All right, I'll stay in the library."

"See you there." He turned around and began to leave. "If I'm late, don't leave," he said, putting one hand on her shoulder. "All right?"

"All right." She had calmed down a little.

On the way home, Jim told her not to worry. He had noticed, too, but he was definitely sure Richard had a very good reason.

"I know," she said, her voice getting emotional again, "he's changing. He's now confused about me."

"About what?"

"About how can he get away from me"?

Jim laughed loudly. "Oh, Sheila," he said, "That's why you were crying?"

The tears ran down her cheeks.

Jimmy got his answer. "I can assure you that can't be possible. You still don't know Richard, my sweet little sis; he's a rock—rock."

"How do you know?" Sheila asked.

"All my life I've known him. And you have to learn to trust him, too."

"Then what should I do?" she asked quietly.

Jimmy looked at her again. "Well, that's something you'll have to figure out for yourself. Be a big girl." He stopped the car in front of her house.

"Would you like to come in?" she asked.

"My wife is waiting for me," he said with a smile.

"Oh, I'm sorry. Thank you, Jimmy." She left the passenger seat and turned to go.

Jimmy got out of the car. "On second thought, let me see Uncle Scott."

They went inside the house. Sheila knew Jimmy well. He always liked to have a cup of tea. So she went into the kitchen to make one for him.

Jimmy stayed for a while, finished his tea, and made Sheila promise she wouldn't go out for the rest of the day. "Just get some rest. Tomorrow you'll be ready for school. Maybe I'll drop you off there before I leave for the hospital."

"Whatever you like, sir." She smiled a little.

"Promise?" He was not smiling.

"Promise!" She looked at him, and then he left.

Sheila didn't go to her room or try to sleep because she knew she'd never be able to rest. She'd only end up being more upset. She helped her father with his paperwork, went into the garden, and spent some time pruning the flowers and shrubs. She liked doing those things. Then she made an early dinner and had a good talk with her father. After all that, she was pretty tired. She went to bed and fell asleep fast.

The next morning she felt refreshed and was able to think about things calmly, fairly, and honestly. She was still in bed and remembered everything. For a while she was very disturbed. Then she turned to the other side, and her thoughts changed, too. *Richard has a strong and solid character; there must be some reason. I shouldn't force or bother him. I think I should leave him for a while so he can get away from his problems, whatever they are; I won't go to the hospital until he comes to me. Maybe I'm bothering him too much.*

"But why isn't he telling me?" she asked out loud. "What's the problem? He looks very worried and disturbed, tired and busy. Why? Why doesn't he tell me anything, especially me! He promised we wouldn't hide any secrets from each other. Then why is he doing this to me?" *Is he changing his mind?* She thought for a while and shivered. *No, it can't be happening. I'm not going to think like that*, she reassured herself.

She got up and started working. She tried to keep herself busy, but she couldn't keep her mind off Richard. Every night she was so tired that she fell asleep quickly. Days were passing. A week had gone by, and she hadn't seen Richard. She wanted to see him. Her heart was telling her to call him.

No, there's no use. She changed her mind and went to change her clothes, then had breakfast with her father.

Mr. Scott had to do some of his own work for a while, so he went into his library. Sheila went to the backyard. The weather was beautiful. She sat on a bench and started reading a book, one she had started reading almost a week ago. She always did that whenever she was disturbed and didn't feel like reading textbooks. She tried to read good novels to get her mind off her troubles. She was absorbed in this book but was almost finished with it.

A car pulled into the driveway. She looked up then pretended to read again. Richard got out of the car. For a while he stood there, trying to get her attention. She finally looked up, and Richard opened his arms to her. She stood up. God knows she wanted the same thing. *But no, I have to keep my pride*, she thought.

"Hello, how are you?" was all she could say.

He dropped his hands and walked slowly toward her. "How are you?" He smiled a little.

"All right. So do you want to see Daddy?"

"Is he home?"

"Yes. Come on."

"First I want to see you," he said as he put one hand on her shoulder.

"Oh," she mumbled.

Richard went with her and sat on the garden bench beside her. Both were quiet. Richard looked as if he was trying to think of a way to start. She was worried. Why, she didn't know. After a while Richard looked at her.

"Sheila."

"Yes," she answered slowly.

"I need your help," he said.

"My help?" She looked at him, surprised.

"Yes."

"With what?"

"With some patients in the hospital," he said.

All of a sudden, Sheila got up. "You just want to use me. I'll never let you do that."

"Sheila!" Richard said. But she ran into the house, went to her room, and closed the door. He smiled, sat quiet for a while, and then came inside the house. He thought after a short talk he would take her and go back to the hospital. Mr. Scott was in the library. He walked in there.

"Hello, son. How are you?"

"All right. How are you, Uncle?"

"I'm fine. Trying to catch up on a lot of things. Oh yes, one more thing to catch up on. Do you know Sheila's birthday is next week?"

"Yes, I remember," he said brightly.

"I want to celebrate it. You know I missed her birthdays the last couple of years," he said, taking a deep breath. "I want to make up for everything."

"I'm very glad to hear that—may I help you in any way?"

"Yes, of course; without you, how can I make it successful? Son"—he put one hand on his shoulder—"you see, her mother and I used to do everything. This day is very special for us—I mean, for me. Well, she's not with us anymore. But we'll try to make Sheila happy, and you're the most important part in it."

"I'm very glad to hear you feel that way. I'll do anything I can to make it a good birthday. And Sandra and Jimmy will help us, too."

"Yes, of course."

"May I ask you one thing?"

"Of course, son. You can ask me anything," Mr. Scott said as he put his arm around Richard's shoulders.

Richard wanted to ask if Sheila's birthday celebration could be a surprise party. But he hesitated. He didn't want to interfere.

"Yes, tell me. What do you want to know?" He was looking at him with devotion.

"Oh, I was thinking how lucky I am to have you."

"We all are lucky to have each other, son, very lucky."

Richard waited for quite a while, but Sheila didn't come out of her room.

"Where's Sheila?" Mr. Scott asked. "Does she know that you're here?"

"If you'll excuse me, I'll go see her." He got up and went toward her room, and after a little knock, he pushed the door. The door was unlocked, but Sheila was not there. He walked around the house; at last he went into the kitchen but couldn't find her there, either. Richard was very disappointed. Then Mr. Scott came in.

"Did you find her?" he asked.

"No. She left to go somewhere, I think."

"That's surprising; she always tells me before she leaves. I think you two missed each other."

"I think so, too. All right, I think I should leave now."

"All right," Mr. Scott said. Then he asked, "Son, do you two have any problems?"

"No, not really. I was too busy, so I didn't call before I came here."

"I see," Mr. Scott said. Both men were intelligent and gifted academically. But there was a difference between them. Mr. Scott had a very hot temper. And Richard was a very cool-minded man. He always thought first, and then acted second.

Whatever happened that day, when Sheila left the house without telling anyone, Richard was very upset and worried. He shook hands with Mr. Scott and left himself. He went to the hospital, gave some instructions to the other doctors, and then called every place he could think of to try to find Sheila. At last he called Jim's house. Thank God, no one was there. Otherwise, he would have had to give at least ten answers to Jimmy.

Where could she be at this time? He thought. *I hope nothing happened to her.* He called a couple of close hospitals. There was no trace. He left the hospital and started looking in the stores, the park, and some walking paths. After a long time, he looked at his watch. *Oh, it's ten thirty. She should be home by now.* Without thinking, he went to her house.

He parked the car and was about to go inside and ask for her. *But no, if she's not there, then Uncle will panic, and I have to have a good explanation for that, so before I go, I'd better think of a good excuse.* He started walking toward the back of the house. Hoping maybe the back door would be open so he could go to her room or to the kitchen.

The weather was nice. The sky was clear, and moonlight flooded the back garden.

He took small steps, thinking to himself, both hands behind his back. His tie was loose, the first button on his shirt open. The cool breeze moved his hair.

There were a couple of benches, chairs, and a canopy in the back garden. He walked straight to the chair and stopped. Sheila was sleeping on the chair, alone! The breeze was making her cold; she had wrapped her hands tightly around herself. Her hair fell on her face, and the signs of tears made her look very sad and innocent.

Richard forgot everything and looked at her for a while. Then he tried to pick her up and take to her room; his eyes were still on her face. The attraction of his eyes, or their hearts' connection, caused her to wake up. She opened her eyes widely.

"You!" She stood up. "What are you doing here?"

"Looking for you. And what are you doing here?"

"I live here." She was fully awake now.

"I know that, but right now it's almost ten forty-five. This is not your bedroom."

"But…" She tried to walk away.

Richard grabbed her by the arm. "Sheila, I'm tired now, so please."

"I don't care."

"You have to. I have been looking all over for you, and you're hiding here. What's the matter with you?" He shook her shoulders a little

"Go!" He was just staring at her. Sheila looked at him closely; he looked tired, exhausted. She couldn't move.

They looked at each other, and Richard said, "Well, go to your room, and make sure to stay there, so I can have some peace of mind at least."

"Well, why were you looking for me?" she asked.

"From past experience, you always get upset over a little thing and get hurt, is that right? I don't have the stamina right now to face any other problems," he said, still angry.

"Did you have your dinner yet?" she asked slowly.

"Did you?"

"No." She looked at him and got the answer; he was starving. "Would you like to eat something with me?" She was looking down, maybe feeling sorry for him.

"I'd love to, if you promise to cooperate with me."

She nodded her head and motioned him to come inside.

"Oh, I'll be here. You go and bring something back."

"Will you wait?"

Richard smiled at her. She looked so innocent. "Yes."

When she came back with a tray in her hand, she saw he was sleeping. His eyes were closed, and he was leaning back, one leg crossed on top of the other. He had folded his sleeves up and wanted to have some fresh air, so he had opened a couple of his shirt's buttons. He had one hand across the top of the bench, his tie was very loose, and air was moving his hair. He looked so different. Sheila had never seen him like that. She watched him for a moment, and then put the tray on the table. *What should I do? Wake him up or let him rest?* She felt sorry. *I'm not leaving him alone here*, she thought and sat beside him, then put her head on his shoulder very lightly. A hand moved across her shoulder. *Oh, he's awake*, she guessed.

"I'm sorry," she said slowly.

He didn't answer. After a little wait, she looked up; his eyes were still closed, and he hadn't moved. She felt his hand on her shoulder. She tried to sit up straight. "The food will be cold. Come on; let's eat." He didn't move, and his hand pressure kept her in place.

"Why did you do that?" he asked.

"Because…"

"Yes?"

"Because—I thought—you were fed up with me, and your attitude was changing."

As she said the words, she felt his hand pressing harder on her shoulder.

Then he buried his face in her hair. "Never think like that, ever. I can't function without seeing you."

"But you were not accepting my help," she whispered.

He sat straight. "Sweetheart, I'm a doctor. My responsibilities are taking care of others, too. I can't take your advice in my field."

"But—"

"But you get suspicious very fast. If you were in my place, what would you do?" he asked.

"Same, I think," she said.

"Good. There will be nothing to come between us. No matter how busy we are." He squeezed her a little. She looked at him, and they both smiled.

"Let me get out of here," he said.

"Please eat first," she said very politely.

He saw her face and noticed she was looking at him. "He said slowly," I am very hungry and so you are, she looked at him again. He saw her and without saying anything started eating. She promised to see him the next day.

The next day, after class, Sheila went straight to the hospital and to Richard's office. She was very curious to know about the case he was working on. After a while she asked, "So, what do you want me to do?"

He turned toward her. "What, sweetheart? What did you say?"

"Do you want me to do something?"

"Yes, I do. I'll tell you in a minute." He bent his head down and leaned back on the chair. She didn't want to disturb him again, so she started reading her own book. After a long time, he stood up and walked around the room, trying to figure out something. He walked slowly to her side as she watched him quietly.

He stopped right beside her. "Sheila, let me ask you something, before I tell you what to do."

"All right," she said, closing her book and sitting up straight to listen to him.

"Do you remember when your mother died?"

Their eyes met.

She took a deep breath and said, "Today is exactly two years."

He turned back and took a few steps. "Exactly. Do you remember what kind of dress she was wearing?"

"Well, yes; she had a pink dress on. But why are you asking all these things all of a sudden?" She was feeling something inside about her mother. *Something is wrong somewhere, why is he asking so many questions about my mother?* She thought.

But Richard was unaware of her thoughts. He questioned her again.

"Did you see that before she left the house?" He didn't give her time to answer. "And do you remember what she had on when her body was identified?"

"It was pink, too, but very dirty and stained, mixed with blood."

"So you can't say that it was exactly the same dress."

"I think so, because the accident happened the same day. How could she change so fast? But why are you asking all these questions? Please tell me something!" Now she started getting in a panic.

"Oh, this case is very similar to your mother's. She looks the same."

"But you didn't see her," she interjected.

"I saw the pictures, and I saw her briefly a couple of times, too."

She didn't say anything; she just wanted to see this woman as quickly as possible.

"Who's she and where is she? I want to meet her, now. Please, Richard." She stood up and held him by his shoulders.

Richard ignored all her questions and said slowly, "She's the one who has no memory. Remember? I spoke with you a couple of times."

"Yes, I do remember, very clearly. And you promised I could help you."

"That's why I wanted to talk to you first."

"All right, I'm ready. I'll do whatever you say." She was excited to follow his lead.

Before taking her, he instructed her on how to act. "One more thing," he said, before leaving his office. "Don't mention anything to Uncle Scott, because he has new eyes. We don't want to put him under any strain that can affect his vision."

"I know that. I won't say anything, until—"

"Until what?" He stopped walking.

"Until I find out for myself," she said slowly.

"Sweetheart, your mother is dead—"

"Don't say that! Maybe—maybe…" She was hesitating to say it, but her heart was telling her that lady had some connection.

Richard could read Sheila's face. He drew her close to his chest; she put her head on his shoulder, closed her eyes, and then took a deep breath. After a while she raised her head. "Let's go now. I'm ready."

"Are you sure?" he asked.

"Yes, I am, and I'll help you, whoever she is." They started walking down many different hallways then reached the patient's door. Before they stepped inside the room, they looked at each other. Richard tapped Sheila on the shoulder and stepped in with a bright smile and new hope.

"Good morning!" he said brightly. The lady was sitting in the chair; the same picture was in her hand, and she raised her head.

"Good morning," she replied. Then she sat up straight, looking at Sheila's face.

Sheila was stunned to see the lady in front of her. She was very surprised, happy and emotional. She wanted to run and go to her, shake her badly so she could remember everything, so she could remember her. She wanted to tell her that she was her mother. But she couldn't do that because Richard was holding her hand very tightly.

"How are you?" he said again, ignoring everything. "My fiancée is here today to meet you."

"Sheila!" Her lips moved slowly, but her eyes were still on Sheila's face.

And God gave some strength to Sheila; she gathered herself and moved toward her.

"Good morning, ma'am. I'm Sheila Scott."

The lady stood up fast and stayed right in front of her for a while without saying anything. Then she moved her hands slowly and held her by the shoulders tightly.

Richard stood right where he was, just watching them. Sheila didn't move, waiting for what the lady would do next.

After a while she started pressing her fingers into her shoulders, and all of a sudden, she drew her in and hugged her tightly. Sheila wanted to do the same thing. They clung to each other. The lady was sobbing. Sheila couldn't stop herself. Tears flowed from her eyes, too. And Richard was very impressed with Sheila's self-control and support for him, which he asked her to do, so he didn't interfere at all.

After a while the lady held Sheila by the shoulders again and moved away a little. "I'm sorry," she said slowly.

"Sorry for what?" Sheila asked impatiently.

"To disturb you. I don't know why I was crying. Why do I get disturbed, whenever I see your picture, and you?" She looked at her again.

Oh, Mommy, it's because I'm your daughter! Her brain said to her. Her heart wanted to say the same thing, but she couldn't say that.

"Oh, maybe you know someone like me. Like a daughter," Sheila said slowly, looking at her face for some sign of recognition or emotion. But there was none.

"I wish I did," she said sadly and lifted her shoulders. "C'mon. Sit here—if you have some time, we'll talk about—about something, about each other."

"Sure, of course," Sheila said.

Richard watched quietly. He interrupted the conversation, saying, "All right, I think you two are quite busy with each other, so I'll leave you for some time."

"Thank you," Sheila said with mixed feelings.

"But I'll see you before dinner in my office at seven. And you"—he pointed to the lady with a smile—"before that."

He left, and Sheila spent almost an hour with the lady. She tried to ask all different kinds of questions to find any clue for herself or some opinion of her memory, but she couldn't find a good solution.

When Sheila returned to Richard's office, she had become upset. That lady looked just like her mother, except a little weak and exhausted. Her hairstyle was different, and of course she was in the hospital gown. Everything was disturbing to think about. *Who is she? Is she my mother? Then whose body was that?*

Sheila's brain was exhausted. She told Richard everything she was thinking and feeling. Richard said, "We have to help her, whether she's just a patient or your mother. We have to bring her memory back first and then find out who she is. Right, sweetheart?"

"Yes, I'll help you and her, as well as myself." She looked at him. "Thank you for letting me help."

"And thank you for helping me," he said, bending toward her with a very bright smile. "I hope we don't have any more misunderstandings."

"Not at all." She tried to smile. "I'm sorry. I was wrong." You were doing all this for me, and I was so—so upset, hurt, angry, and disappointed that I couldn't explain to you," she murmured slowly with her head down. But Richard paid attention.

"Tell me, why were you doing all those things?" He came closer to her.

She looked at him. "I told you."

"What?" He pretended that he didn't know.

"That, I thought, as a matter of fact, I was almost sure that you were fed up with me, until—" She stopped again and looked at him.

"Yes."

"Until Jimmy assured me."

"About what?"

"That—that, you're a rock—nothing to worry about that. You two have known each other since you were children."

"Yes, that's true."

"I want to know a little more about you two, please," she said, looking anguished.

Richard looked at her then looked in the space

"His father practically raised me. Jimmy was always a naughty child, and I was quiet, but we liked the same things.

So we were always together. Went to the same school, college, and then were apart during medical school. He was admitted here, and he was happy because Uncle was alone. I had to go to a dorm because my dad wanted me to have some experience. We both applied to the same schools, but we were admitted at different places. We stayed in touch, sometimes helping each other study. When we finished medical school, Daddy appointed both of us residents at his hospital, here. Jimmy was happy to be here."

"And you?" Sheila asked with interest.

"I was, but"—he inhaled deeply—"I didn't want to take on all the responsibility. Especially watching Daddy's bad health. Jimmy was always my right hand. He always encouraged me, helped me, gave me advice when I was in a tight spot—even when he had problems, he stayed upbeat."

"Yes, yes, say all the bad things about me to my sister." Jimmy rushed into the room and sat beside Sheila then looked toward both of them. "Am I interrupting anything?"

"No," both said in unison, "not at all."

"OK, you two can complain about me. I'm here only for a couple of minutes." He put his head back and closed his eyes.

Richard and Sheila both smiled and went back to their books and files, while Jimmy stretched out his legs and started to take a little nap.

Sheila said very slowly, "Please forgive me."

Richard looked at her, smiled, and nodded his head.

He didn't say anything. He just gazed at her, then said in a very deep and slow tone, "I need you and your help always, sweetheart. I want you with me always. The question is when, where, and how. I hope you understand."

"Yes, I do—I do," she said in the same tone.

"Right now, I think Uncle Scott needs your help." He stood up with her.

And Jimmy was sound asleep. They left the room quietly.

9

When she came home, she was extremely happy. She knew that the woman in the hospital was her mother. She had found her. She wanted to scream, dance, and jump for joy, but she couldn't do any of these. *Daddy does not need to find out like that, at least not in his condition—especially since he's recovering himself. Yes, of course, I have to wait for them. They both have to recover their health. That's what Richard wants, too.* "After all, he's the one who's doing all this," she thought and the words came automatically out of her mouth aloud.

"Doing all what?" Mr. Scott asked. He was going by in front of her room when he heard her voice and came inside to verify.

"Doing everything, up to now, you know. I was so blind not to understand both of you, but why are you asking that? She looked surprised.

"Oh I just heard you were murmuring some thing, 'Doing everything'".

"Daddy, I'm sorry, so sorry." She jumped up and came to him and put both arms around him. She tried to change her words to whatever she had just said.

"That's OK, honey, but why are you so excited and talking to yourself?"

"I was?" She surprised herself.

"Or maybe I'm thinking so much these days," he blamed himself.

"What are you thinking these days, Daddy? Is there a problem?" Now she was worried about him.

"No, not a problem, just a thought."

"Do you want to share?" she asked.

"Nobody can help me now. It's over," he said, taking a deep breath and turning to leave her room.

"Daddy, may I ask a question?" She looked at him.

"Sure, honey. You can ask anything." He stopped and looked at her. "What's the question?"

"Daddy, do you miss Samantha? Do you want me to call her for you?" Her head was still down.

Mr. Scott stayed quiet for a while as usual then turned toward her and said in a deep, low voice, "I miss your mother, my wife. Now no one can help me. She's gone, forever, and I'm alone because I don't have the same feeling for anyone, not even Samantha." He turned again to leave her room.

She didn't want to force him. Sometimes she was still scared of him; even his attitude was completely changed now. Her happiness was a little bit shaded, but then her thoughts came back around to her mother again. *I'll take care of her. First I have to think about her. She's my mother—I'm very sure—but who was that died that night? Daddy identified the body.* Images of that night flooded her mind. But there was a gap in the middle. *When I went to identify her body, after seeing the pink dress, I screamed, and the police kept me away from her. They had a conversation among themselves; I was sitting in a separate room.* Then what happened? She didn't know.

Yes, I remember Daddy took me back home along with the police. I had a very bad headache. I think I threw up on the way back. We came home. "Mommy," I was murmuring. Then Daddy took me to my bed. He sat down with me. After that, everything was over. I don't know. I don't remember. Now I think I've found her. What should I do? Or maybe she just looks like her. That could be possible, too. She started confusing herself again.

"Dinner is ready," Mr. Scott called from the kitchen. She came back to her senses. "Coming, Daddy!" She started moving toward the kitchen and thinking, *whoever she is; first I have to help her get her memory back.*

The next morning, she was feeling much less stressed. She took a shower and got dressed. *When Mommy was around, she never liked me to go out without taking a shower, dressing properly according to the weather, and having a little freshen-up.* She dressed exactly the same way today. *I don't have any classes in the morning, so I'd better go to the hospital first.* The urge was provoking her. She came out of her room, and Mr. Scott was reading the paper.

"Good morning, Daddy," she said.

"Good morning," he said, putting his paper aside. "Oh, you're ready already?"

"Yes," she said.

"Doesn't your class start in the afternoon today?" he asked.

"Yes, first I have to go to the hospital to help them." She always liked to mention Jimmy and Richard. Jim rarely needed her help, but she liked to mention both of them. "Then I'll go to my class. After that, if you need me, I'll come home. Otherwise, I'll go back to the hospital again because they're very busy these days."

"I know that. They're always busy, something new all the time," Mr. Scott said.

"They take each and every case very seriously."

"Oh, I think someone is blowing their horn! Go, honey. Have a good day; I think this is Richard."

"I think, but—" She wanted to ask something.

"Go first and ask later." He pointed toward the door. "He's waiting for you."

"Bye, Daddy," she said and ran outside. Jimmy was there.

"Good morning," he said through the car window.

"Good morning," she said and sat in the seat beside him. "Sandra didn't come today?"

"She doesn't go to school anymore," he answered with a casual smile. Sheila suddenly remembered that Sandra had graduated. "Oh my God, I forgot—totally."

"Anyway, only your brother cares about you." He laughed and looked at her.

"Thanks." She was smiling, too. Both were relaxed and in a good mood. They were quiet for a while, deep in their own thoughts.

Sheila was happy but confused. *What should I do to bring my mother back to my life? What if she remembers, and they find out that she's not my mother?* She shivered to think that.

Jim was surprised to see her shiver and started asking questions. "What's the matter? Are you sick? Why are you shivering?"

She was worried and confused but still 90 percent sure the patient was her mother.

She looked at Jim. "What? Excuse me?"

"Now you can't hear very well, either. I think you have an ear infection." His eyes were still on the road, so she couldn't see the expression on his face.

"What are you talking about?" she asked, looking at him. "I don't understand."

"I said"—he bent toward her a little—"are you all right?"

"Yes, I'm all right—but…"

"But what?" he asked.

"My brain is not," she murmured.

"That I know," he murmured back.

"What do you mean?"

He didn't answer, just looked at her quickly. She saw a mocking smile on his face.

"Are you teasing me?"

"Not at all." He looked back to the road.

"Then why did you say that?"

"Saying what?" The car was running fast, and so was her temper. She didn't say anything. Whenever she was very angry or confused, she stayed quiet. That's what she did now. Jimmy was used to her anger. After two minutes passed, he asked again, "Why are you quiet now?"

"Because I don't like you," she said sharply.

"That's OK. Here's the hospital," he said.

"Thanks," she said and opened the door.

"One more thing," he said.

She didn't answer, just paused before getting out.

"Don't take out your anger on that poor man."

"And don't come to pick me up again," she said as she got out of the car.

"I will," he winked, as the car started moving and so did she.

When she went to Richard's office, he was waiting for her, in a hurry as usual.

"Good morning. I was waiting for you. Let's go," he said.

"Go where? I just got in; I'm not going anywhere." She sat down.

"Why? Didn't you get a good night's sleep? Happy, sad, why are you uptight? It's just morning," he said, smiling a little.

"I wasn't, just—Jimmy made me angry.

I'm a good girl, and he's the bad one." Jim came into the room.

Sheila grabbed Richard's arm. "Let's go. "He got up quietly, made a little turn and waved his thump up towards Jim. Both smiled and Richard left with Sheila.

After they had walked a little way, Richard asked, "Where are we going?"

"To see Mommy," she said quickly. "I mean, that lady."

"Oh, let's go, then," he said.

"I hope you do not have to go somewhere else?" she asked.

"That's OK. I have to go in the same direction anyway."

"You were in a hurry this morning. I'm sorry; I should have checked with you before leaving," she said.

"I have a meeting about that matter. So I wanted you to visit Ms. Anna."

"Ms. Anna?" She looked at him with surprise and happiness.

"That is her name," Richard replied.

"All right." She started running toward her room, waving her hand. "Thank you. Attend your meeting. I'll see you, or you can pick me up from her room."

"All right." Richard waved back then headed off in the other direction.

By the time she reached Anna's room, she was breathing hard. Her face was red, and her feelings were very mixed but positive. She took a moment at the door to calm her.

"Sheila, wait." Jim was approaching her. "What's happened now? Why are you so much happier?" He was coming to see Anna, too. Every morning he checked on her as he had promised Dr. William, and at least twice a week, Jim talked on the phone with Dr. William and let him know the latest condition about Anna. Dr. William was a very good person. He wanted to keep in touch with Anna through Jimmy because she was not in a condition to talk with him. Jimmy also knew the story about Sheila and her mother, which Richard and Jimmy both wanted to keep secret until she got her memory back because they were still not certain about her identity.

"I'm not happier; I'm excited. She's my mother. Jimmy, I found Mommy." She put both hands on his shoulders, forgetting their quarrel.

"How do you know?"

"Because her name is Anna—Anna Scott," Sheila said.

"Anna Scott? But how do you know?"

"Richard just told me!" She shook him a little.

"Richard told you her name is Anna Scott." He repeated everything. "Let's go inside. I have to see her chart." He got a little excited, too. "But wait." He stopped her before going inside.

"Why?" She looked at him.

"We don't have to tell her anything. We want her to remember herself," he said.

"Yes, so?" she asked, puzzled.

"So, take a deep breath, calm down, and walk like a normal person," he said.

"I can't do that. I feel like running straight into her arms. I feel like telling her everything. I feel like talking—and talking."

"And I feel like sending you home without seeing her," he said, pushing her hands back.

"Why?"

"Because you're out of your mind," he said.

"Why?" She stared at him, looking puzzled.

She was quiet for a moment and looked down. "You know…" She looked back to him.

"What?" He was looking at her, too.

"You're a good brother, and a very good friend, too," she said, smiling but with tears in her eyes.

"I'm your brother; that's right," he replied, then joked, "But…" He waved his hands. She turned toward his hand. Richard was coming along with another doctor. Jim joined the team. Sheila was just standing there between Richard and Jim, listening to their conversation. Finally, they all went into the room.

Anna was sitting on a chair, looking as though she was waiting for them to come in and still holding the picture in her hand.

"Good morning!" Richard went to her first and shook her hand.

Then Sheila said good morning and approached her. She opened her arms and hugged her.

Jim said hello, and Dr. Bernard introduced himself. Anna nodded, but her eyes were on the picture and on Sheila's face.

They talked to one another casually and tried to include Anna in the conversation. At one point, Sheila couldn't resist asking, "How do you know that your name is Anna?"

"Dr. William told me that my name is Anna "

"Did he tell you your last name too?" Sheila asked.

She stayed quiet for a minute then shook her head. "No."

Dr. Bernard was watching her quietly. Then they all left.

Dr. Bernard was the best, Jimmy said.

"I'm very much satisfied now," Richard said.

"Meaning?" Sheila asked.

"Meaning, after Dr. Bernard's visit, his decision will be the best and last."

"Do you know him?" she asked.

"Daddy knows him," Jim said.

"'Daddy?' You never mentioned your father before."

"Well, I have to have a father. What do you think?" He looked at her with a smile.

"I don't mean that," she said.

"What are you two arguing about now?" Sandra asked when she cames in the room.

Jim said, "Oh, I'm just teasing her, she's so—"

"OK, let's get back to important things," Richard interrupted.

Sandra wanted to go to the library with her so Sheila could finish her assignment before taking her class. Sheila wanted to do the same for her class. But instead that she joined the meeting with Jim and Richard. All three went to the conference room and sat down.

"May I have a cup of coffee, please?" Jimmy asked, looking at Sheila.

She looked at him with an empty and confused look. Richard looked at her, too. His heart ached when he saw her innocent confused face. She looked upset, completely lost.

"Oh, I'll make it." He moved from his chair.

"Don't worry; this is my job," Jim said as he stood up. "I was just trying to—"

"Make her more confused," Richard answered with a smile.

Jim realized what he meant and said in a low tone, "Sorry."

Coffee was on the table. Sheila had a cup, but she didn't touch it. Richard started talking.

Sandra joined them later because she wanted to take Sheila back to the library. They had an understanding: if Sandra didn't push her, she would not finish her class requirements because of her family's situation. So Sandra had come to pick up Sheila, but got stuck in the discussion about Anna's new treatment.

Dr. Bernard recommended to Richard and Jimmy that her new treatment should be in a different environment, a home environment. Not in the hospital. "She's not sick, and she does not need more medicine," Dr. Bernard said. "She needs a home."

"She can go back to Dr. William," Sandra suggested.

"No, not at all. She's not going anywhere! I don't want to lose her again—never!" Sheila yelled.

"OK. We don't think so either," Jimmy said.

"I'll be happy to give her a home. But I don't have anybody there—except—because of Uncle Scott, Sheila can't help her either," Sandra said again.

Richard spoke slowly, "Someone has to give her a home."

"I think so, too," Jimmy said. He put his pen down on the table and leaned back. "But the question is, where will she have that type of environment?" Richard's voice vibrated.

"We can create one." One doctor said.

"Create one?" Sandra couldn't stop herself, as usual. She didn't usually attend doctor's conferences, just the regular staff meetings. But Jimmy and Sheila wanted her to join this one because Sandra was very much involved in this particular case.

"We have to do something to bring her memory back," Richard said again in a strong voice, looking at Sheila.

She was sitting very quietly, not interfering, but her mind was working very fast. She didn't want Anna to go anywhere. She certainly didn't want to burden anyone. She didn't want to lose her mother again, but how? She couldn't bring Anna to her house; Dad was home after his new eye operation. *I don't want to take any chances with him. After all, I needed his sacrifice so much, and how much can I test him to prove his love? How much? But I want both of them. I have to! I have to!* She looked up, and the room was empty. Her thoughts were so long, deep, and personal that she didn't realize the conference had ended and everyone had left.

"What's happening? Where's everyone?" she said as she stood up.

Richard was searching for something; he looked at her calmly as usual. "The conference is over; she's still in the hospital in her room, and I'm here, starving," he said.

"What did you decide?" She ignored him totally.

"We'll discuss that later; let's eat something first."

"I'm not hungry."

"I was waiting for you," he said, looking at her.

"Then why didn't you go?" She was totally lost.

"I had to look for something, and now I'm finished, so let's go." He shut the computer off, gave her a glance, and started walking. He knew what was on her mind.

They walked to the restaurant, where Jimmy and Sandra were already sitting at a table for four. "Did you check the menu?" Richard asked Jim.

"Yes, I did, and I ordered for you, too."

"Thanks."

A menu was sitting in front of Sheila, but she didn't touch it, just sat quietly; physically she was there, but mentally she was far away.

The food came, and the waiter came to her after serving everyone. "Anything for you, madam?"

"Huh?" She looked at him blankly and then came to her senses. "Oh, a yogurt, please." She was still looking in the air.

"Thank you," the waiter said and was about to go.

"And an empty plate, please," said Richard. They started talking generally, to change the mood. The waiter came back with a cup of yogurt and an empty plate. Richard took the plate, put some food on it, and served it to her without the yogurt. She saw everything with an empty mind and started eating like a child, without saying anything. Nobody was saying anything to her, nor was she participating in any of the conversation; everyone knew her very well, and if she was thinking or disturbed, it was best to just leave her alone. Jim wanted to say something, especially when she asked for a yogurt, yet she was eating the food without talking or saying anything. Richard was just relieved that she ate her lunch.

"Sir, do you want something more?" the waiter asked.

"Oh no, thank you. There was a lot of food here." He showed his empty plate with a smile. Jim and Sandra had to laugh.

Sheila looked at everyone and started laughing, too. She looked at Richard and asked, "Did I eat all your lunch?"

"Half, but I had a yogurt, too," he said.

"Do you want some more?" She was concerned now.

Before he replied, Jim said, "I ordered for two, so let me ask you, what have you been thinking since the conference room?"

"About Mom," she answered quickly.

"May I make a suggestion?" Jim became professional and glanced at everyone.

"Yes." Sheila looked at him, and so did Richard and Sandra.

"If Richard approves, we can talk to Dr. Michel and make an appointment for Uncle Scott, and he can make up a story about his eyes. Tell him he has to wear a bandage, or dark glasses, for a week or two."

"Why, is anything wrong with Daddy's eyes?" Sheila interrupted. She looked completely confused.

Sandra started smiling, and Jimmy was about to say something, but Richard knew she was scared, tired, and had so much to handle at the same time.

"No, nothing is wrong with him," Richard said. "We just want to make up a story so he can have his dark glasses, so Anna could be in your home."

"Home," she said, very slowly.

"We hope so." Richard stood up, and so did Sandra and Jimmy. Sheila was still sitting. Richard was looking at her, thinking maybe she wanted to talk more, or maybe she wanted more to eat. He looked at her, waited, and then they looked at each other.

"We've sat long enough," Jim said. "We have to leave now. Let's go, come on!" Jim tapped on her shoulder lightly. "I have to make up a story." In his mind he knew that Richard wanted to stay and comfort her, but he didn't have time.

"Oh, thank you, Brother"—she stood up—"and thank you, too," she said, looking at Sandra. She looked towards Richard and noticed he was looking at her too. They gave each other a knowing glance, a little smile. Then they all went their own ways.

Sheila wanted to talk with Sandra; she wanted to understand Jim's thoughts, and she definitely wanted to be with Richard. She wanted to be with him as soon as possible—to calm her mind and to let him console her.

But he's busy right now. I can't bother him all the time. After all, he's doing so much. I can't bother him, she said to herself. She got up, thinking that she would go home and rest.

A hand came around her. She turned her face. "Shall we?" Richard asked as he tightened his arm around her shoulders.

"How did you know I was here?" She was surprised and happy.

"I—I smelt your fragrance." He bent his head to touch her neck.

"Come on. Tell me isn't this the time you make rounds in the hospital?"

"Which I did—half," he said as they walked.

"And the other---half?" she said in the same tone. Because she was so happy to see him, she forgot her tension for a while.

"You look happy to see me, hon."

"Yes, I am." She leaned a little toward him.

Richard looked at her, and they both laughed. "The other half Jim will take care of."

"What time do you have to go back?" She knew he was a busy man.

"I can stay as long as you want me," he said, looking at her.

"Thank you so much! I very much want to be with you," she said.

"You got me—a long time ago."

"I'm proud of myself."

They needed no words. Both kept quiet and kept walking. "Where are we going?" she asked.

"Home. I want to see Uncle Scott." They stood by the car. Both turned to move to their sides to sit down. Richard's voice vibrated in her ear, "Sheila."

"Hmmm?" she whispered, without looking at him.

"When I talk to Uncle Scott, please help me out," Richard requested. They were so comfortable with each other that there was no formality between them. Like opening the door or always saying some words to prove to each other how much they loved each other or any other unnecessary emotional approach. They were just honest, open, and truly faithful to each other.

"OK, but how do I know what your motives are?" She was still looking straight ahead.

"Meaning?" He turned to look at her.

"I mean, how do I know what you're going to talk about?" She looked at him.

"I'm going to talk to him about his eyes. And I will try to convince him. So please do not interfere in the middle. He looked at her and started the car.

She was still looking at him mindlessly.

"And you need a good rest. So please have one." The car was heading toward her home.

A little while later, Sheila said softly, "Richard."

"Hmmm?" he whispered back.

"May I ask you a question?" She was still looking at him; he looked so handsome, strong and energetic, she lost herself. "I still don't understand."

"What?" He was still looking straight ahead.

"How come you love me?" She felt as if she were talking to herself.

But he heard her whisper. He stopped the car in front of her house. "What—"

"You're way ahead of me."

He looked at her for a while; his glance was so deep that Sheila lowered her head. Then she heard him laugh, very hard. She had never seen him like that—happy. He looked so charming; she just kept looking at him. Then she said slowly, "I mean it."

"Shee!" He put his hand to her mouth to make her stop.

"You should see yourself through my eyes. Sweetheart, you have a lot of talents, and you're a very intelligent and beautiful girl, with lots of problems. And that's why we're trying to solve them."

"We?" she asked.

"Jimmy and me."

"I know he's really a good brother; he helps me a lot. But what about you?" she asked.

"What about me? I'm fine, absolutely happy, particularly to be with you." He looked at her with a little surprise.

"I know, but you're always involved in my problems. You have your own life, too," she said in a very low tone.

"To me, we're made for each other," he said. "Whatever we are, it's a one-to-one situation, and Sheila, your problems are mine as well as, I think."

"Of course," she said.

"So let's come and solve one first." He was still smiling.

She looked at him and wanted to say something. But he spoke first.

"You know what? Your silly talk and this innocent face"—he touched her cheek with his hand—"make me feel even closer to you."

She gave him a look of appreciation and opened the door.

Mr. Scott was sitting on his patio, reading the paper.

"Good evening, Uncle," Richard said to him.

"Good evening, son. How are you? Good to see you, but at this time?" He was surprised. "Did you see Sheila? She's not home yet."

"I'm here, Daddy." She went into the house with a couple of bags, things she had bought before the hospital meeting.

"Oh, so you both were shopping?" Mr. Scott guessed.

"No, I bought these things before meeting them; I'll be in the kitchen."

"How are you doing, Uncle?" Richard asked. "I came to see you."

"I'm perfectly fine," he replied, putting the paper aside. "Do you know I like to read and try to keep myself busy? But my eyes get tired sometimes. I think they're still healing."

Richard was grateful for the opening. "Let me see," he said, as he checked his eyes. "I think they're a little bit red, too. I think I'll make an appointment with Dr. Michel, and you will have a checkup."

"Whenever you want, son. I'll be there."

"Let someone pick you up. Please, don't drive yourself," he said.

"Perfect," Mr. Scott said. "Did you two eat, or will I have to fix something?" he asked casually.

"I think Sheila bought some groceries. We'll have dinner together," Richard said. "Let me help her." He went into the kitchen.

"Daddy, did you have your dinner already?" Sheila shouted from the kitchen. Her mood was completely changed. She had some hope now, and Richard was with her, which always made her feel good.

"No, not yet, honey," Mr. Scott, said.

"Then the three of us will have dinner together," Richard said again.

"Do you need my help, Sheila?" Mr. Scott asked his daughter.

"No thanks, Daddy."

"I'm here, Uncle. Don't worry," Richard said. As they made dinner, Sheila saw that Richard was very comfortable in the kitchen.

"I hope you're not torturing yourself in here," she said, looking at him.

"Not with you," he said with a smile.

"And what do you do when you're at home?" she asked.

"Miss you and try to keep busy," he said.

"I mean, do you cook for yourself, or does your house-keeper make it for you?" she asked.

Her tone was very casual. Richard looked at her face then said, "Most of the time I have dinner before going home. Sometimes if I want to eat at home I call my house and ask them to fix my dinner for me." He talked as he worked.

"But you cook so well. I think you're hungry, hon." She smiled at him.

"Yes, I am."

"OK, sit down here." She pointed toward a dining chair. "That way we can talk and you can relax a little." He looked at her and kept working. "I'm hungry, and I think four hands are better than two, hon."

"I think you're right. I'm hungry, and I think Daddy is, too."

"Let's get this done. We can talk later," he said, starting to wash a couple of dirty dishes. Sheila gave him her father's apron. Richard thanked her. Sheila noticed that he seemed at home in the kitchen. In a way, she was happy to see that. Richard noticed that she was looking at him and smiling. As he put food on the table, he asked, "I know you were laughing at me. May I ask why?"

"Oh, I was just surprised to see you like that. I mean, cooking—like that."

"Sweetheart, I was in the dorm for a long time, since I never had a mother, my father wanted to teach me everything and prepare me for anything."

"Sorry to hear that." But you look so tired, I think you should have some rest."

"I'm rested. You know why?"

"Why?" she asked.

"When you're doing something you enjoy, your mind relaxes; you feel happy; you're energized; and you can work fast, accurately, and efficiently." As he talked, Sheila felt close to him and wanted to spend as much time with him as possible.

Then she smiled and looked him in the eye. "So you gave this speech of yours about cooking, not about medicine?"

He said, "Yes, now call Uncle so we can have dinner."

"Dinner is ready, Daddy," she shouted from the kitchen.

Mr. Scott came to the dining table, looking very pleased to see them happy together. *If my observation's right, they will be a remarkable couple. But I'm going to miss my daughter—very much. My house will be completely empty, and God knows what I'm going to do alone. Without her and without her mother and. She was the best company of my life. She left me, and she'll never be back.* He inhaled deeply. *They're happy. So am I, and the rest I'll deal with later.* He was thinking, and Sheila and Richard were watching him and waiting for him to come back from his thoughts. Finally, Sheila looked toward Richard, who was so hungry. Now he had to wait while Daddy was deep in thought.

"What are you thinking about, Daddy?" she asked.

Mr. Scott came back from his thoughts. "Oh, it's nothing. I'm just deeply impressed to see all the food you've prepared."

"Thank you, Daddy," Sheila said.

"Shall we start?" Richard looked toward both of them.

"Yes, of course," Mr. Scott said, and they started eating and talking. Mr. Scott wanted to know who had cooked what.

"We cooked everything together," Sheila said. "Richard is a good cook. Really, I was surprised."

Richard ate quietly. Then he asked, "Do you like everything, Uncle?"

"Yes, everything tastes very good. Imagine, a doctor who can cook."

Richard laughed. "Doctors can cook many different things, Uncle."

"I understand that, and what are you working on these days?" Mr. Scott asked pleasantly.

"These days I'm working with a woman in my hospital who has lost her memory. No one came to claim her, and we don't want to let her leave like that.'

"So how long will she stay in the hospital?" Mr. Scott asked.

"Uncle, actually she's a very good woman. Her brain is perfectly all right, she talks perfectly, and the medical staff thinks she needs a home environment." He looked at him with a little hope.

"I'm sure you'll cook something up," Mr. Scott quipped.

"We will," he said, looking toward Sheila. Both smiled slightly, and Sheila got up to wash the dishes. Richard and Mr. Scott kept talking—about the past, the future, politics, culture, what they liked, what they missed the most. Sheila got a little emotional when her father talked about her mother, about his regrets. Richard listened and tried to understand him better. It was a wonderful dinner and a successful meeting with Mr. Scott.

10

The next morning was a new day. Mr. Scott agreed to use dark glasses for two weeks. Nature was helping them. Bed rest was recommended because he never stopped reading, writing, or doing some work to keep himself busy. Sometimes he bent his head without realizing it, even though he knew he shouldn't bend his head after his big eye operation.

In spite of everything, he sometimes forgot those important instructions. It was fortunate for him that he did not develop any problems in his eyes though he definitely did not want to lose his sight. "I had a very depressing and boring period of times in my past. Now I'll do whatever is important for my eyes," he said to himself. "That's why he returned home with dark glasses."

And Mrs. Anna Scott returned to her home without a memory, money, or name. She was only Anna, a stranger.

It was a big day for Sheila. She was very excited, very joyful, and her heart was pounding. *Finally we're together. Well, at least under the same roof. I don't have to run around searching for them.* But one corner of her brain was asking her, *what's going to happen if she's not really my mother? What's going to happen when Daddy takes off his dark glasses? I hope this will not hurt his eyes. And what's going to happen if Anna's memory does not come back? Am I going to take care of her—in this house—whether she's my mother or not? Would staying in the house for two weeks bother her, too? What's going to happen after two weeks?* She wanted Anna to continue living with her. She wanted to continue her education. All sorts of questions were coming to her mind and puzzling her all the more.

Her father came home and went to his room to rest. Because of his dark glasses, he was unable to read, watch TV, or do anything. Besides that, he was a little bit depressed. But he wanted to follow the instructions because he didn't want any more problems with his eyes.

Anna stepped into the house without knowing anything. At the time of her discharge, she had asked, "Where's Dr. William? I don't see him? Where am I going?" Actually, she was a little scared.

Sheila had stepped up beside her. "You're coming with me." She smiled and went closer to her.

She looked at her and kept looking for a while. "Who lives with you?" Anna asked.

"It's just me and my father," Sheila answered.

"You don't have a mother?" She looked surprised.

"Now I do," Sheila said pleasantly.

"I know! I'm *like* your mother, but—"

"But nothing. I'm very happy right now. Please don't ask questions."

Anna stayed quiet for a while, and then said slowly, "Sorry."

And that's the way she arrived at the house after her discharge from the hospital. She was sitting in a room with Sheila and Sandra, very quiet, thinking something, looking around the room, turning her head with surprise; sometimes a little depression showed on her face.

Sheila and Sandra were talking to each other, discussing school schedules and the hospital, their work, how busy they were, all sorts of things. They showed no sign that they were both there to take care of two people and keep them separate in the same house. That's why Sandra decided to stay with Sheila, at least for a couple of days or until the situation improved. Because Sandra was a newlywed, Sheila didn't want her to stay. But Jim and Sandra didn't listen to her, and Richard was very pleased about that.

Sheila watched Anna intently, without her noticing that she was being monitored. She just tried to be helpful or talk. Sheila listened very carefully. If Anna said anything or did something unusual, Sheila would very carefully write it down. She made sure that Anna took her medicine and rested. She worked to make sure the house was a pleasant environment.

This was a start for Anna and an exam for Sheila. *A good result will benefit me rest of my life, she* thought.

"What are you thinking about?" Sheila asked and came to her.

"Nothing much. I was just thinking about my job," she answered slowly.

"I don't understand what do you mean," Sheila said.

"Let's go. I'll show you some parts of the house, as well as your room."

"I'll have a room, too?" She was a little excited.

"Sure, everybody has their own room." Sheila held Anna's hand.

"Good. Sandra will stay, too?" she asked. By now she knew Sandra and Jimmy very well.

"For a couple of days," Sheila said.

"Why?" Anna asked.

"I'm in college," Sheila said, "so we have to work together."

"I see," Anna said, looking a little confused.

They walked toward Anna's room. Sheila entered first to welcome her; then Anna was in the room. "Beautiful," she said. "Everything looks so perfect. Who decorated this, you?" She looked at Sheila.

"Yes." Sheila nodded her head. Her eyes filled with tears because she had decorated the room according to Anna's taste. She fixed everything, every color and design, the way she used to like it. That's what Dr. Bernard had asked her to do so he could observe her reaction, and maybe it would help bring her memory back. Sheila's heart filled with joy to see that Anna appreciated everything.

"It looks like I decorated the room. Our tastes are exactly the same," she said.

"I know. I can see that!" Luckily Sheila had marvelous control over herself.

"If it's possible, I'd like to get some rest now." She wanted to go to bed early. Maybe she was feeling tired or depressed from being in a new place. Or could it be possible that after seeing her dream room, she felt the way she used to, and that was comfortable. It was hard to figure out. But Sheila didn't ask anything.

"Of course, please take a rest. By the way, do you want to have dinner?"

"No, thank you. Not at all," she replied.

"Good night." Sheila hugged her and left the room.

In the morning, Mr. Scott and Anna both got up at the same time. Mr. Scott used to wake up in the early morning, get ready, and go to the kitchen to prepare breakfast while Sheila got ready. Every morning they had breakfast together, washed the dishes, then said good-bye to each other and followed their own schedules.

But this morning, Mr. Scott woke up as usual, lying in bed, thinking about how he was going to spend the day. He heard the sound of dishes from the kitchen. *Sheila must have woken up very early.* He got out of bed. He was allowed to take off his glasses to go to the bathroom, take a shower, or any place where there was not much light. He was not allowed to put pressure on his eyes. So he couldn't do much until his next checkup.

He looked at his eyes while shaving; his eyes were fine. "I don't know what Dr. Michel is saying. They look all right to me," he said to himself in the mirror. *Anyway, I have to listen to him sakes of my own health.* Then he put the dark glasses back on and went into the kitchen.

"Sheila! What are you doing up so early?" He was standing at the kitchen door. "You know what? Let me help you. Dr. Michel asked me to use these glasses outside, not in the kitchen." He put his hand up to take off his glasses.

"Good morning, sir. Sheila is still in bed. May I wake her up?" Anna said.

"Good morning. I'm sorry to disturb you." Mr. Scott's hand came down from his glasses. "Don't bother; thank you." He left the kitchen and sat in the chair on his porch. He turned on the radio to listen to the news and weather.

"Good morning, Daddy," said Sheila.

Sandra was there, too, and said, "Good morning, Uncle."

She was not ready yet. In the morning, she took her time; they walked around, had breakfast, talked to each other, and discussed their schedules for the day. That way if she had to make any changes, she would be able to do so.

Sheila did the same thing, but first she got ready.

"Good morning, honey," Mr. Scott said and raised the volume on the radio a little to listen better.

"Where's Anna?" Sandra asked Sheila.

"Where's who?" Mr. Scott turned the volume back down.

"Anna," Sandra repeated.

"Oh, this lady's name is Anna, Daddy."

"Really…Her voice is very much the same, too," he said.

"Really? Do you think so, Daddy?" Sheila asked with excitement. "When did you hear her voice?"

"I thought you were in the kitchen," he explained. "I'm sorry to disturb her. If I knew I would not go there." He looked at her.

Because of his dark glasses, she was unable to read his facial expression. But she felt a little scared as usual and said, "Sorry, Daddy. Everything happened so fast that I forgot to ask you."

"About what?" Mr. Scott asked. Then he replied, "I know that Richard was cooking something while we were eating dinner last time." A little smile was on his face, which Sheila could see.

"Oh, you're not ready yet," Anna said to Sandra. Sheila heard and made a turn to the kitchen.

"Good morning. I'm ready," Sheila said with smile.

"Good. Breakfast is ready. Please forgive me; I made it without checking with you."

"Without checking what?" Sandra asked. "And I like to get ready *after* breakfast," she explained, politely.

But Sheila understood what she was talking about. "I'd love to have whatever you made."

"Come and have your breakfast," she said as she stood up. Mr. Scott was listening to the conversation quietly. Then Sheila came to walk him to the table for breakfast.

Tears came to Sheila's eyes. Everything was the same—same taste, serving style, and the way she was looking at her. She felt the urge to hug Anna.

Mr. Scott was very quiet during breakfast. Sandra observed everything, while enjoying the excellent meal. It was rare for her to have that type of treat.

"I knew that I did something wrong," Anna said, feeling sorry.

"No, not at all! Everything is so perfect, after so long, that tears came to my eyes." Sheila was wiping her eyes and smiling.

"Really?" Anna looked happy.

Mr. Scott couldn't stop himself. "Thank you—Anna, everything is marvelous. Actually, it's the same like before, and that is her reaction, as well as mine, too."

Anna understood. "Thank you, sir." Then she looked at Sheila. "I think your mother used to cook that way."

"Yes." She nodded her head.

Mr. Scott and Sandra got up. She had to get ready and leave for work.

Sheila and Anna were alone in the kitchen. One was remembering everything, and the other was just feeling sorry for her.

"Have some more. You hardly ate anything." Anna said to Sheila.

Mom use to say that, too, Sheila said to herself, or *maybe it is in my mind too much; that's why I feel like that*.

"You miss your mother so much?" Anna asked.

"Yes, but how do you know?" she asked, looking at her.

"About what?" Anna asked, a little surprised.

"That—that I miss my mother."

Anna got up, took a deep breath, and came close to her. She put one hand on her head and bent a little to look at her. Sheila was watching her, comparing her action to her mother's. They were the same. The two women looked at each other very closely. Sheila was still quiet, looking at Anna and watching her actions and hoping, maybe, she would remember something. But there was nothing, except sympathy.

"Your face always tells me everything, dear. And maybe I have a daughter like you—somewhere." She stood up. "Come on. Finish your breakfast and get ready for the new day."

"New day," Sheila repeated.

"Of course, I'm here, so you don't have to worry about housework, at least for a while," Anna said, smiling.

"Why for a while? Why not forever?" She stood up. "I won't let you go anywhere until you remember everything."

"I do –I do remember things. I just don't remember my past," she said.

"I know, and that's what I'm talking about. You know, you have to remember your past. About yourself, your family, and your life. Where you came from. But you have to work for that, too." She came right up to her, very emotional.

Anna didn't say anything; she just looked at her very closely. Sheila felt a little glimpse on her face, a true feeling, inner emotions and a motherly love for her. Sheila was getting excited also, and then she suddenly sat down in the chair, quietly.

Sheila got scared. "Are you all right?"

"Yes—yes, I'm just thinking; what should I do to remember my past? You know I want to. Sometimes I think maybe I have a family. Someone I know…somewhere."

"I'm sure, too," Sheila said. "And you know what? I'm sure you'll succeed one day. But right now, I think you should rest. I think you're tired after all this." She looked around the kitchen.

"Yes, I think I should," Anna said and tried to get up. "But let me straighten up a little first." She picked up the dishes from the table.

"Oh, I'll do that. I always help Daddy, too." She looked at her intently. Anna looked back with a bright smile. Sheila saw very clearly love and affection in Anna's eyes. But she tried to avoid that and asked, "Did you have breakfast yet?"

"Not yet," Anna said.

"Then you should have your breakfast first, and I'll wash the dishes."

"I think you should finish yours, too."

"All right," she said and sat down. Both finished their breakfasts and cleaned the kitchen while talking about different things. Sheila was trying to gather ideas from her so she could compare similarities. She also had a feeling that

Anna was talking naturally and was handling the kitchen as she used to. Sheila remembered so much of her style. Anna worked without even thinking. Sheila was afraid to leave her alone, so she passed the time until Sandra finished her work. Sandra and Sheila had set up a schedule so that one of them would be in the house at all times. Sandra had to juggle going home, going to the hospital, and visiting her mother.

After cleaning the kitchen, Anna asked Sheila when she would be leaving.

"In a while," she said. "I have to see if Daddy needs me."

"All right, I'll be in my room."

"See you later. Remember to take your medicine," Sheila reminded her.

"Do I still have to take medicine?"

"You know what?" Sheila came into the room with her. "Let me check with Dr. Bernard; maybe he will recommend that you also take some vitamins, which you can take in the morning, and this one at night."

"Check first," she said, just like Anna Scott, and lay down in the bed.

Sheila went to her father's room to visit him. He was lying straight on his bed, looking at the ceiling without his dark glasses. Sheila sat beside him. "How are you feeling, Daddy?" She was trying to be pleasant.

"You're still here?" he asked.

"I'm waiting for Sandra to come," she answered.

"Why?"

"Because we decided to take care of you with your dark glasses, as well as Anna, too."

He looked at her, absorbed her happiness, and wanted to say something but stayed quiet for a while. "How long is she staying?" he asked slowly.

"Dr. Bernard wants to observe her situation for at least two weeks," she said.

"What situation?" he asked.

"They want her to have a home. So she could feel like a normal person. Also, she will continue her medicine, and hopefully she will get her memory back."

"What? You mean she does not have a memory?" Mr. Scott was very much surprised.

"I'm sorry, Daddy. I was so worried and busy that I forgot to discuss her condition with you. She does not remember her past." A thought came quickly: *I hope he does not kick her out again.* "I think Richard was mentioning that last night at the table." She tried to remind him.

"Oh yes, I remember," he said slowly. "That's all right, honey; you're a big girl now. And very intelligent, too." He looked at her. "Your decision is acceptable."

Sheila could not believe her ears. *Is he the same person?* But that's OK. He had changed for the better. She looked back at him with appreciation.

"Do you think I should let her stay as long as she needs to?" she asked, fearing he would say no. If he said no, she did not know what she would do.

"How long has she been sick?" Mr. Scott was trying to figure out something, too.

But Sheila didn't want him to build false hope, so she said, "I don't know for how long, and we can't question her very much because she gets a headache."

"I see," he said and started looking up at the ceiling again.

"That's all right. I'll let her go to some other house," Sheila said.

"Oh no, let her stay here; that's all right, honey. She just reminds me of your mother so much."

"I feel the same way too, Daddy," she said, touching his hands.

"And that's why we'll let her stay," both said at the same time. Then they laughed.

Sandra arrived, and Sheila left the room. Sheila told Sandra what she had observed about Anna, including her conversation and actions. Sandra reminded Sheila to hurry so she wouldn't be late for class.

"Oh, my schedule is changed now. I don't have my class until this afternoon," Sheila said.

Sandra looked at her smile a little and said, "I think you have to go anyway because someone is waiting for you." Then she went to her room, and Sheila looked out the door. She saw that a car was waiting for her.

"Good afternoon," Jim said.

"Good afternoon," she said, looking at her watch. "It is noon already. You're here again!" she exclaimed, and she sat in the car.

"That's my job, dropping one off, and picking up the other," he joked, and they both laughed. All the way they had a good conversation about Anna and Mr. Scott, and lots of different little things.

At one point Sheila was surprised and said loudly, "Jim, where are you going?" She saw they were going in a different direction.

"Brother," he corrected her and kept driving.

"All right, Brother," she repeated, "where are we going?"

"I'm sorry, I forgot to ask; do you have anything important to do? Your class or hospital obligations?" Jimmy looked at her quickly.

"No...but maybe Richard is looking for me."

"He knows," Jim said, still driving.

"He knows what?" Sheila was a little surprised.

"That we'll be a little late," Jim replied.

"Why?" she asked again.

Jimmy stopped the car in front of a house and looked at her. "Once you were surprised that I have a family."

Sheila remembered her words saying, "You have a father, too!" Jim had ignored her question and made a joke, saying, "Well, I have to have one."

"Yes," she said.

"I want you to meet my father today. After all, you're my sister; he should be related to you, too." He looked at her. "At least morally, you and I are related. What do you think?" He looked very sober, very graceful.

"Yes, of course," she said. "But I met him during your wedding."

"Yes, but not quite, because you were with Sandra most of the time, and you met my father only briefly."

"That's true," she said.

Both opened their doors from their sides to get out. There was a single house in a good and quiet neighborhood. Both were quiet in their own thoughts; they walked together. Jimmy opened the front door and held it for her to come in.

"Daddy!" he called his father. It was the first time she had heard him call someone his own father.

"Jim, are you here already?" His father's voice was very similar to his. Jim kept walking up to the kitchen table, obviously familiar with his father's place. He stood up. "You're with another girl!" he said with a sweet smile.

"Yes, my sister, Sheila," he answered with a proud voice, "and Sis, this is my daddy, Mr. Tom Bradley."

"Good afternoon, sir," she said politely as she raised her hand to shake his. A very nice and charming man was standing in front of her, very much like his son.

"Good afternoon, honey," he said, coming closer to her and giving her a light hug instead of shaking hands. "Jimmy mentions you a lot," he said.

"But he—" She was about to say; "never mentions about you" but stopped herself.

"But she does not know about you," Jim said.

"I know. How could she?" Mr. Tom said slowly. "Come on, Sheila. Sit down, and have lunch with us."

"Thank you, sir, but—"

"I'm hungry," Jim said, "and Richard has a lunch meeting."

Sheila didn't say anything; she just sat down. Jim was walking around the house, and Mr. Tom and Sheila were talking about a variety of things, nothing personal. She liked him; his son was just like him. Mr. Tom was working in the kitchen.

"May I help you?" she asked. Jim came back from some corner of the house and started doing things; he knew what to do next.

"That's all right, honey," Mr. Tom said.

"We don't take help from a stranger," Jim said.

"Well, I'm your sister, so this is my house, too," she said, and she started bringing food to the table. Lunch was simple but tasty and delicious. Sheila asked who cooked the food.

Jimmy replied, "Me, of course," and he looked toward his father with a bright smile.

"Right, of course. You can cook something medically but not the food. I don't believe you," Sheila replied.

Tom smiled and then said slowly, "I've been cooking for so long that it has become my hobby, working around the house all by myself. And you know, it makes the time pass quickly. When I go to bed, I fall right asleep."

She thought about how hard it was for her to fall asleep. Her mind was always crowded with thoughts. She turned from side to side in bed and in the morning felt miserable.

Sheila felt sorry for him and said, "Uncle, if you want, I can help you. I help Daddy every day in the kitchen."

"Thank you, honey, but as I said, I'm used to it now, and when Jimmy is around, he helps me."

When they were finished with lunch, she helped clear off the table. Then she asked Jim to take her to school for her class.

He looked at his watch. "Your class will start at three p.m., and right now it's only one thirty. Do you want to go now and wait outside the classroom or at the gate?"

"Or maybe in the library to finish my assignment," she said.

Tom was listening to their conversation and said, "It's good to have you both here. Wait a little while, honey."

"Oh, I can stay, Uncle, for half an hour more. These days I don't have time to finish my homework at home, so I go to the library and study."

Jimmy said half an hour was enough time to make tea.

On the way, she told Jim how pleased she was to meet Uncle Tom. "But it's surprising that you never mentioned him before." She looked at him.

He gave a quick glance. "The subject never came up."

"That's true; I'm too involved in my own things. Would you like to talk about your mom?" she asked.

"What about her?"

"Where is she? How is she? When will you take me to meet her?" She asked so many questions at once.

He smiled a little. "For that we have to go to her, because she's not coming here."

"What do you mean? I don't understand." She thought he was making fun of her again.

But he stayed quiet for a while then said slowly, "She left me."

"When?"

"When I was born," he said slowly, not looking at her. "I don't have a mother, sis, she's dead."

Sheila felt sorry she had asked him. She bent her head for a while.

"Uncle Tom never married again?" she asked slowly.

"Never. He raised me all by himself," he said…as if he were talking to himself.

"Must be hard for him to go to work and—"

"My father is a writer, Sheila," he completed her question. "He writes in magazines, papers, and he's written books, too, to make his living, as well as mine, in the beginning. When I started school, then he started working, and that's where he met Uncle Scott."

"Daddy knows him?" She was surprised to hear that.

"They're office colleagues," he said.

"I never saw him," she said.

"Mostly Uncle Scott used to come to my house."

"I can remember." She was thinking how scared she used to be; mostly Mom and she were alone together. He had his own pride, hobbies, work, and stubbornness.

"What are you thinking about?" Jimmy looked at her.

"I'm wondering when you saw me for the first time? Because Daddy never took me with him to your house; mostly I used to stay with Mom."

"I saw you so many times on different occasions, especially when your mom died and you were sick. Somebody had to be with you while Uncle Scott and my father went back to the hospital."

"I see." *That solves one mystery*, she thought.

"And since then, I've had a sister." He looked at her. "At least I feel that way."

"Because you feel sorry for me?" she asked.

"Because I see you in the same boat," he said quickly.

"Thank you, brother." She was impressed. She stooped for a while purposely.

Then asked slowly.

"When did you meet Sandra?" she asked without looking at him. Actually, she just wanted to change the conversation.

He smiled a little, kept looking ahead, and kept driving, then said, "This is a tough question. You two are friends. I'm sure you had a conversation on that subject."

"Yes, we had a little," Sheila, said.

"And that little information is not enough for you?" He looked toward her.

"Oh, I wanted to hear both sides of the story." She looked at him also.

He smiled brightly and said, "Some other time. Right now you will be late for your class."

She looked at her watch and thanked him.

"You're welcome," he replied as he stopped the car in front of her college.

In the evening, she went to the hospital to visit Richard. He was waiting for her. He looked a little tired, sitting in his office on the sofa with his tie having been loosened, trying to relax and read a magazine.

"Good evening," Sheila said and sat beside him on the sofa.

"Hey," he said and put the magazine down.

"Were you waiting for me? You look tired," she said.

"Yes, I was waiting for you, and I'm tired, but right now I'm hungry, so let's go," he said as he started to get up, then stopped. "How are you? And how was your meeting with Uncle Tom?"

"Very good," she said and got up.

"And how are both my patients—under the same roof?" He looked at her with a little concern because they both had brought Anna into Mr. Scott's house without his permission. They knew that wasn't right. They knew that Mr. Scott's feelings could get hurt. But all three of them— Sheila, Richard, and Jimmy—had had to make that decision to give her a nice home and observe her changes. They didn't have any choice, so they played all those games. But inside, they were afraid of the potential consequences.

"As a matter of fact, both your patients are very well so far," she said.

"Good to hear that." He felt relieved. "Let's go." He got up again.

"You should eat something, and I was thinking of going home. Maybe Mom and Daddy are waiting for me," she said.

"Do you want me to come, too?" he asked.

"Of course, but you look tired; maybe you haven't eaten for quite a while," she said, and tried to force him to eat.

But Richard had his own idea. He was walking toward the car. "We have to wait for food anyway, and it's better to wait a little more for a homemade dinner," he said.

Sheila didn't answer; she just felt sorry for him. He liked the home environment. She gave him some mixed nuts, which they nibbled while he was driving. Sheila held the nuts in her open hand. She was very relaxed and had pleasant thoughts.

"What are you thinking about?" Richard asked.

"About Uncle Tom and Jim," she said.

"Did you like him?"

"Yes. Jim took me this afternoon to meet his father." Sheila was still holding the nuts in her palm.

"He's a very nice man." He took some nuts from her hand while driving.

"I think so too, but it's surprising that I just met him for the first time."

"You saw him before; you just didn't get a chance to meet," he said pleasantly.

"Really? How do you know that?" she asked with a smile, too.

"Because I saw you." Richard was totally enjoying himself.

"You're just teasing me. No more nuts—starve," she said and closed her fist. The car stopped in front of her house.

Richard turned his face to her and held her hand. "Fine, I'll eat your fist."

This is a different Richard, the real one, mine, she thought and lifted her hand up while opening the door.

They both got out of the car and walked into the house, where Anna was sitting at the table and Daddy was walking on the porch, a little uncomfortable, thinking of something.

"Good evening, Uncle," Richard said, as he walked to him and shook his hand.

"Hello, son. You're here just in time! I know your patients are here and you wanted to check," Mr. Scott said.

Richard understood the hint but ignored that, because he got a little scared at first.

"What's the matter? Is she all right?" he asked.

"Yes, of course. She's taking care of everything. It looks like I don't have to do anything now."

"It's good, Uncle, because these days you're not supposed to work anyway," Richard said quickly.

"Yes, I know that. I was just saying that she's taking care of everything very well, just like—" He stopped for a moment, took a deep breath, and said, "before."

"But is she doing anything against your will, Daddy?" Sheila asked.

"No, honey; that is the problem. She's taking care of the house just like my Anna used to. I don't want to get involved with this woman. Her not having a memory is challenging me."

Sheila looked confused. Her father's dark glasses were off. Both were home most of the time. And it was very difficult for them to not notice each other. She was wondering what she should do.

"I understand your concern, Uncle, and that's why I'm here to visit both of you."

"There's nothing wrong with me; I just had my full checkup yesterday."

"I see. Good to hear that your eyes are fine now," Richard said. "Let me have a visit with Anna."

"Sure…why not?" he said and sat in the chair with his paper. Richard was a little confused, too. He went into the kitchen, where Sheila was putting away the groceries, and Anna was helping her. She seemed to know where everything went. Richard watched her quietly. He was surprised to see this new Anna, fresh, healthy, happy, and completely the opposite from who she was at the hospital.

"Oh, Richard," she said when she saw him. "I mean, *Doctor* Richard—why are you here?" she asked as she stood up and looked at him.

"To see you," Richard said, "and Uncle Scott, too."

"Oh, so you know him?" she asked, a little bit confused.

"Yes," Richard said, and an arm came around him.

"Does he know me? Let me introduce him to you. He's my son-in-law-to-be," Mr. Scott said.

Sheila kept quiet.

"Oh my God, it means you're his—fiancée!" She pulled Sheila into her arms. And Richard stood with Mr. Scott.

"Yes," Mr. Scott said, "and I'm the lucky one to have them both." Mr. Scott's mood was changed completely.

"Of course," Anna said in a low voice. "Congratulations."

"Thanks," Mr. Scott said, without looking at her. But Richard and Sheila both noticed her inner pain.

Sheila turned toward her. "May I call you Mom?" She looked at her with tears in her eyes. "I don't have one."

Both were looking at each other for a while with tears.

"Yes—yes, of course. My heart is telling me I have a daughter like you—somewhere."

"We'll find her. But meanwhile, you just relax and feel at home, take your medicine, and rest," Richard said.

"Then?" Anna questioned.

"Then you will have your memory back," Sheila and Richard both said together.

"And I'll meet my family?" she asked.

"Yes" Sheila said.

"I do not know how long it will take" She looked at them.

"Do not worry about the time," Richard said.

"If it is all right with Mr. Scott." She looked at him, and at the same time—for the first time—Mr. Scott's eyes met hers.

"Anna." He had taken one step forward with his eyes fully open.

Sheila and Richard both were alert for this new development. Sheila was scared, but Richard's face was calm as he watched carefully.

All of a sudden, Mr. Scott bent his head down and turned back. "No—no, it's not possible; my Anna is gone.

This is not she—it's not possible. She's someone else. This is not she. She can't be; I'm sure." He kept walking, and Richard followed him.

Anna sat on the chair, very quiet, thinking.

"What are you thinking about?" Sheila asked as she sat beside her. "Are you all right?"

"He looks very familiar. I think I saw him somewhere."

"I'm sure you did. Could you think where?" Sheila asked,

"I don't know, but I know one thing: I should leave now."

"No!" Sheila said quickly, looking at Richard's face. He just came back from the porch, where Mr. Scoot sat in a chair with his eyes closed, Richard saw him and turn back to kitchen.

"We have to discuss that first; you see, I'm your doctor, and health comes first."

"I'm all right. There's nothing wrong with me except my memory," she said.

"And sometimes you forget some recent events, too," Richard said.

"Like what?" She looked at him.

"Like when we met for the first time, meaning you and me." He put his hands on her shoulders.

"Yes, what's the connection with this?" she asked calmly.

"At that time I showed you Sheila's picture and—"

"Yes, I remember," she said slowly. "Right now, I totally forgot."

"And that is the most important thing. I won't let you go without knowing who you are." Richard was trying to handle things professionally.

"I know, but I saw Sheila's mom's picture in her room. And Mr. Scott's tension is right. I don't want to disturb him, his feelings, or his home life."

"We thought about that," Sheila chimed in. She had come back after seeing her father, who was sitting quietly with his eyes closed, and she didn't want to disturb him.

"Don't worry about anything; you do whatever you're doing for her"—Richard pointed toward Sheila and touched her shoulder—"and for yourself."

"Yes, Mom, please," Sheila said as she held her shoulders with her hands. And Anna held her hands in hers.

"Let's have dinner," Richard said. "It's way past dinnertime, and I'm starving."

"You've been hungry for so long!" Sheila stood up with smile.

"I think everyone is, right Aunty?" He looked to Anna.

"Yes, it is very late, she said then stood for a while and looked towards Richard. Both were looking at Anna and waiting, maybe she remembered something. But she said to Richard with smile and "I know that you two are engaged "I was just trying to make her father happy."

"But you just said that you forgot," Richard said, puzzled.

"To make you happy." She laughed.

"That's very nice of you," Richard said. Then they started talking to each other's in a low tone just to change the atmosphere.

Anna watched both of them and could see they were happy. She stood up to help out the food at the dinner table.

Richard was a completely different man. He was young, determined, active, and pleasant. Sheila had never seen him that happy. Her headache was a little less, and then she remembered her father, who was a sad and lonely person. Somehow her heart ached for him.

Anna was confused by the contrast between Sheila and Richard's happiness and Mr. Scott's sadness. *What should I do, leave for his convenience, or stay for them?* It was hard to decide.

"Mom, we're hungry," Sheila said loudly. Mr. Scott heard her.

He opened his eyes, got up from his chair, and started walking slowly toward the kitchen.

"Come on, Uncle, we're starving," Richard said as he saw him coming.

The kitchen table had four chairs; three people sat, but the fourth one was empty. Anna was thinking about stepping outside the kitchen. Everyone noticed, and Sheila held her hand to encourage her to occupy the fourth chair.

Mr. Scott was deep in thought. Sheila and Richard talked to each other, just to keep the conversation going. After dinner, Richard poured coffee for everyone. Mr. Scott said, "I want to say something to all three of you." But he was facing only Sheila and Richard. "Don't change any plans or schedule. Don't leave the house, because health comes first." Both understood whom he was talking to, even though he was not looking in that direction.

Richard said, "Of course. You both are my patients, and I'm not recommending that anyone go anywhere." He looked at both of them.

Anna glanced at everyone and said slowly, "I was thinking that, but I don't want to make a quick decision at this time."

"What?" the three voices said together. Everyone was trying to dig something out of that.

Anna was stunned by the words that came out of her mouth, but she couldn't explain.

"Oh, I'm sorry. I don't know what I'm saying," she said.

"It's happened before, too!" Richard said.

"Sometimes, I say something that I don't know myself. I think you should know that." She looked at Richard.

"Yes, I must say, it's normal," Richard said quickly. "I think whenever you remember anything, even if it doesn't seem important to you, you must try to think more."

"And please, let us know," Sheila said.

"And that way you'll help yourself," Richard explained.

"I think so, too," Anna admitted, "but still—"

"What? 'Still' what, Mom?" Sheila spoke again.

Mr. Scott was listening to everything quietly but didn't want to interrupt.

"I don't know when I'll remember my past, if I even have one." Anna looked very sad. She gave a quick glance toward Mr. Scott. "I want to go back to Dr. William."

"That way you will never remember anything," Richard said quickly, with confidence.

"Why not?" she asked.

"It didn't help you before," Sheila said.

"But I don't want to be a burden to anyone." She glanced toward Mr. Scott again.

He raised his head. "You have full permission from me as long as you want to stay here—with Sheila. It's not a burden." He got up. "Good night, everyone."

Sheila and Richard shook hands with pleasure.

"May I go to my room, too?" Anna asked.

"Yes, of course," Sheila said. "Good night."

"But let me put the dishes away first," she said as she stood up.

"Oh, we'll take care of that." Sheila turned her toward door. "Have a good sleep, and take your medicine, please."

Richard helped Sheila clean the kitchen. After everything was done, Sheila realized he was still in his work clothes; his tie was loose, sleeves were rolled up, and his jacket was somewhere.

"I'm sorry; I didn't realize that you were still in your work clothes."

"So?" Richard looked at her.

"I mean kitchen work and suits don't go together."

"These are working clothes, and I'm working—in a kitchen or a hospital, it's all the same." He was calm as usual, and smiling.

"Thanks," she said.

"Where am I sleeping? I have to get up early."

"Oh, you're staying here?" she asked.

"If you'll allow me," he said, looking at her very pleasantly.

"I will." She was drying her hands. "Let's go see what Daddy is doing."

They peeked into Mr. Scott's room, but he wasn't there.

"Where is he?" Sheila said.

They went to the porch; he wasn't there, either. Usually Daddy liked to go to bed by now. Sheila looked worried, while Richard walked to the library, where he found Mr. Scott sitting quietly with his eyes closed. Richard went slowly inside the library; Sheila followed him. She sat beside him. But Richard was standing and looking at his watch. Mr. Scott opened his eyes.

"Oh, you both are here. How come?" He looked at them.

"It is eleven thirty, so we thought—"

"It's very late. What time do you have to get up?" he asked Richard.

"At five thirty or six a.m.," Richard said.

"I think you should stay here. Just go to bed, son. You need some rest." Mr. Scott stood up. Sheila showed him to his room and gave him pajamas so he could rest.

"OK, Daddy. You go to bed, too."

"Yes, I will."

The next morning, Richard woke up as usual, but he was thinking he should go home first to change and get ready. He got up from the bed and came out from the room. He thought everyone was asleep; he could go to the car just like that, in his pajamas. He heard some noise from the kitchen and thought, *it must be Anna, let's see how she's doing.* He was thinking about her, what could he do to bring her memory back. He was thinking of changing her medicine as he went into the kitchen to see her. But Sheila was already there.

"Good morning," she said. "You're not ready yet! I thought it was late already."

"Good morning. I have to rush." He sat on the chair and started writing.

"You have to rush, but you're not ready yet." She laughed.

"I have to have clothes, darling." He made a face at her. "A shirt, tie, and underwear," he said, lifting his head to give a glance, and kept writing.

"Those I got for you, right there on the table in front of your room."

"Really? But where did you get those from?" He was surprised.

"I'm not telling." She turned her head.

"I think you drove to my home, either late last night or very early this morning." He was looking at her. "You shouldn't do that."

"I didn't," she said, smiling.

"Then?" He was still writing while talking.

"First take a shower, and get ready, and then you'll find out."

"Yes, ma'am," he said and left the kitchen while Anna was rushing in. She heard some noise and rushed to see why everyone was there so early.

"Good morning," Richard said to Anna.

"Good morning, Doctor. You're here early. Is something wrong?" She was surprised to see him in the kitchen so early.

"I stayed here because it was very late."

"Oh, I'm late in the kitchen, too," she said and kept moving.

Richard didn't want to disturb her and went to pick up his belongings, which Sheila got for him. He was surprised to see that she got every necessary thing for him, even a toothbrush. He was very impressed and happy.

Almost half an hour later, after he got ready and returned to the kitchen, everyone was waiting for him.

"Good morning, son. Come on over here." Mr. Scott gestured to the chair beside him. "Did you sleep well?" he asked.

"Yes, very well." He looked happy.

They had a good breakfast that Sheila made. "Everything is perfect," Richard said and looked at Sheila.

"Yes, my baby can cook now," Anna said and gave a motherly look to Sheila.

"You made this breakfast?" Mr. Scott asked her.

"Yes, you thought—" She almost said "Mommy" but stopped. A father understood his daughter's language, though. "Yes, just like that." He took a deep breath.

"I learn from her, though," she said slowly with her head down.

Everyone looked at one another, but no one said anything. Mr. Scott's head was still down.

Meanwhile, Richard talked to Anna about medicine and her health. He told her not to worry about anything except herself for now. Then he wrote down some instructions for her.

"I think it's seven thirty now; you'll be late," Sheila said to Richard.

"Oh, I talked to Jimmy; I'm not in a hurry. Go and get ready," he said to her.

"But I have to take care of this first," she said and started picking up the dishes.

"No, you go and get ready. I'll take care of that," Anna said.

For a second Mr. Scott thought, *I wish I could help her,* but no; he got up and left the kitchen at once.

Sheila left, and Richard helped Anna, even though she tried to stop him.

"You're ready for work. Don't get yourself messed up in the kitchen."

But he didn't listen. "I like to wash dishes sometimes."

"Your mother is lucky to have you," Anna said.

"Yes, I'm sure she would be, but I'm not."

"Why?"

"Because I don't have one," he answered.

"Sorry to hear that. And your father?"

"A couple of years ago he passed away, too."

"I think you need more help than—"

"I'm fine, Auntie; I have you, Uncle Scott, Sheila, and Jimmy, plus my hospital, which keeps me busy all the time." He remembered that he had discussed his past with her before, but she didn't remember.

Or maybe she's saying things purposely. He did not say anything because he wanted to observe her.

After he finished helping, he saw that Mr. Scott was going out, too. He came to Sheila. She was ready, fresh, and looking very smart and pleasant.

"Thanks for everything," he said as he came close to her.

"You're welcome." They both looked at each other. "And thank you for helping us for so long," she said.

"You're quite welcome. I'm a doctor, and this is my job."

"To wash dishes?" She was smiling brightly.

He looked at her while rolling down his sleeves. "Sometimes, if I have to." They both laughed. He was trying to button his one sleeve with his other hand.

She looked at him and came closer to him. "May I help you?" She started buttoning one sleeve of his shirt then the other.

He didn't say anything, just looked at her. Then he said slowly, "In that way you will make me more lazy."

"How?"

"I'm so used to doing all my work by myself."

"Then why are you keeping all those servants in your house?"

"They're here from my dad's time, and I don't want to let them go. They're like family now."

"I know. All three are very good people."

"Are you happy with them?" he asked.

"Yes, they were very cooperative at that time. But what difference does it make? I'm here," she said.

"Yes, but one day you will be there, and I'm very delighted to hear your approval."

"Thanks," she said and saw his face brighten. She was glowing herself.

"Now, tell me, how did you get everything so early?" he asked, looking at her with appreciation.

"My brother helped me."

"Oh, that's why he called me and said that he was early today, so I should take my time."

"Maybe," she said.

"Good." He came a little closer. "You will be a good wife," he whispered.

"I hope so." She smiled at him.

"I know so"—he winked at her—"and I'll see you later."

"Bye, Auntie," he said to Anna. "Uncle Scott is leaving, too."

"Oh, Daddy is going somewhere," she said and understood why Richard was going ahead and not taking her with him.

There was an unspoken understanding between them that someone would be in the house with Anna since she was new here and didn't have memory. She was doing fine, looking great, improving every day, and speaking normally. But still, everyone was conscious of her, hoping to see her health improve and her memory return. Curiosity was killing everyone, including the doctors. That's why when Richard saw that Mr. Scott was getting ready to go out, he let Sheila stay there for a while. He promised to call her back and arrange for Sheila to attend her class.

Mr. Scott had to leave for an important reason. He told Sheila he would be back before noon so she could attend her class. It meant that Daddy also understood Anna should not be alone in the house.

"Thank you, Daddy," Sheila said. She also wondered how Daddy could take care of Mom when he preferred to keep his distance. Sheila looked at her father without realizing he was looking at her and reading her facial expression.

He came closer to her and said in a very low voice, "I keep my distance, but I keep my eyes open."

She looked at him, surprised.

Richard watched them and realized what was happening. But he did not get involved in their conversation. He simply asked, "Uncle, are you driving, or may I drop you off?"

"Oh, I'd love to, but its a little bit out of your way, son."

11

Anna stayed with Sheila and her father for quite a while. She managed the house as if she had never left it—at least that was their observation. Anna was helping around the house but was also trying to keep herself busy. There was no pressure on her. She was totally free to do whatever she wanted. She was taking all her medication and getting enough rest. The chores she did were her own choice. No one asked her to do anything; no one needed her help. But no one had the courage to stop her from doing anything she wanted to do around the house Specially Sheila, Mr. Scott, and Richard—were happy to see her improving health and were waiting to see if she would recover her memory. Jimmy was very involved in Anna's case and tried to help the family as much as he could.

Anna had peace of mind, especially when she was around Sheila. Her health was very good. Life was calm for a while.

Sheila took out her mother's car, which had been sitting in the garage since she had left the house. No one had the courage to sell it or give it away. "Sometimes," Sheila said, "I don't have the heart to give her belongings to anyone. I still feel that she's coming from someplace, any corner of the house, or driving in." *Yes, yes, but she's gone. Face the facts. Try to forget it and resume your present life* Both father and daughter had thought so many times. When Sheila finally came to ask her father for permission to let Anna drive the car, Mr. Scott said yes. He didn't have any hope of Anna coming back. He hadn't given away her belongings because of his daughter's wish. So Sheila gave Anna permission to use the car.

"Do you have a license to drive?" she asked.

"Yes."

"And you're allowed to drive anyplace?"

"Yes, Dr. William was a practical person," Anna said. "And he knew my brain capacity. He gave me permission to drive the car; he thought it was good for my memory and for me."

Sheila said, "I think so, too. I have a car that is sitting in the garage, so you can use it."

"Really?" Anna looked happy.

"Yes. C'mon, take a look." Sheila took Anna to the garage. She opened the driver-side door for her. Anna got into the car and sat quietly for a while, looking here and there, looking everywhere. Sheila walked around and got in on the passenger side. She was quiet, too, missing her mother. But she watched Anna's every move with a smile. She was told to watch Anna's new reactions and make notes, *which I'm going to do later,* she thought.

"What do you think? Do you like this car?" Sheila asked.

"Yes, very much," Anna said.

"Your car was the same?" she asked.

"Which one?" Anna replied.

"Did you have a couple of cars?" Sheila was surprised.

"Where?" Anna looked at her.

"Dr. William's place," she said patiently.

"No, Mrs. William gave me her old one. But this car—"

"What happened to the car? You don't like this one?"

"No—no, I love this car. Feels like this is mine. I saw or used this one, someplace."

"Could be," Sheila said. She continued looking at Anna; maybe a little hope or wish was coming true. She waited a couple of minutes then took a deep breath and said, "You can drive if you feel like it. But where's your driver's license? Do you have one?"

"It was in my pocketbook when I came here."

"And your pocketbook is in your room. I think you should check first."

"Yes, I should. Thank you. So if I find my driver's license, may I drive?" Anna asked as she kept looking around the car.

"Yes, you may," Sheila said.

"Thank you."

"You're welcome. But first let me check with your doctors."

"My doctors?" she asked.

"Yes, Richard and Dr. Bernard."

Anna bent her head and said slowly, "Yes, of course. How could I forget them? Please check with them first, and thanks for everything."

"You're welcome," Sheila said, and they both got out of the car.

The doctors gave permission, and from that point on, Anna drove the car. Her hobbies were very much like Anna Scott's. Even Mr. Scott was noticing now and then. Her movements, the way she took care of the house, even the way she talked were the same.

Sheila was noticing and making detailed notes. She was happy, hopeful, and praying for Anna's memory to come back.

For Mr. Scott, it was very difficult to stay in the same house and avoid her presence. He liked to keep himself busy, so mostly he spent his time in the library, outside, and even in the house, keeping away from her as much as he could.

Anna had a similar situation. She was an active woman. She did housework according to schedules; finished; and then liked to read, write, swim, or even go out, but where, with whom, and how? She did not have much money to spend. She had little cash, which Sheila provided her to use for the house.

Once she went to the library to see if she could find some books that interested her. She walked slowly inside, and then went straight to where Anna's books were on the shelf, found a couple out of order, and put them in their proper places. She selected some books and turned to leave. Mr. Scott was watching her every move. Surprised, he got up with the intention of catching her, thinking there was something suspicious. Anna got scared to see him there when he stood up suddenly from his chair.

"I'm sorry. I didn't mean to disturb you. Sorry, sir," she repeated fearfully a couple of times.

Then Mr. Scott came to his senses. "I'm sorry. I didn't mean to scare *you*," he said. "You can stay; I'm leaving." Then he left the library.

The next morning he was talking to Sheila about re-opening her mother's case.

"What do you mean? Why do you want to reopen Mommy's case, Daddy?" she asked. Mr. Scott told her what he had seen in the library. "Maybe it just happened, or maybe she visited there before and she knew where to go, Sheila tried to explain to him."

"I was thinking that, too," he said slowly, "but we're not losing anything if we just satisfy ourselves."

Of course not, she thought. *He's going to do it anyway.*

"I want to discuss it with Tom," he said and got up.

"You mean, Uncle Tom, Jimmy's father?" she asked.

"Yes. We're friends and office colleagues; he's a very good and helpful man."

"Like Jim," she said.

"No, Jim is like him," he replied with appreciation and pride. "He's an extremely loyal and honorable man."

"I'm sure, but may I ask you something, Daddy?" she said as she looked at him.

"Sure, honey," he said, turning his face to her.

"Uncle Tom and Mommy's case, I don't understand the connection."

"I think you don't remember. Tom was with me when we went to the police station, and then we came home because you were very sick. We came home and left you with Jimmy for almost half a day. Only Tom was with me all the way; he's the right person to ask for help." He got up from his chair. Every morning he sat on the porch and read the paper, since Anna was in the house.

"May I ask one question?" she said.

"Yes, what's your question?" he asked, while picking up his cell phone, glasses, and house keys.

"When did Uncle Robert arrive?"

"They came for the funeral, and Tom was with me when I was alone with the police, with you, with the lawyer, to bring your mother's body from the hospital and all the way along." He looked at her and said, "One thing you should remember: friends are more helpful than relatives in an emergency."

"Thanks for the advice, Daddy. Have a great day," she said, and they both went their own ways.

Sheila walked slowly toward the kitchen. *Let's see what Anna is doing*, she thought, but Anna was standing in her room, very quiet, with her head down. She had a couple of books in her hand. Sheila saw her and felt very sad for her. *She didn't do anything wrong. Why is she standing like that?*

"What's the matter? Are you all right?" Sheila asked Anna.

"I have a feeling that Mr. Scott has been very disturbed since last night," Anna said.

"Yes, something is on his mind; don't worry, he'll be all right."

"Do you know why?" Anna asked.

"After Mommy's death, he got very sensitive about every little thing," she explained.

"But this time it's different," Anna said.

"What do you mean?"

"I went into the library, and I think he got disturbed by my presence," she said and bent her head again. "I should apologize to him."

Sheila saw her face and felt very sorry, but she didn't say what the reason was. "I think he saw you in Mommy's section, and your resemblance disturbed him. C'mon, I'll show you the library," she said as she pulled her toward the library. Then she said, "Let me take these books, too," indicating the ones Anna was holding. They both went into the library. Sheila walked her around to show her where everything was. They put the books in their exact places. "I'm sure you came in here before?" Sheila finally asked.

"No, actually, I never had the courage to go into your father's bedroom or here," Anna said. "But yesterday I was feeling depressed. I didn't know what to do; then I decided to pick up some books and came in without thinking."

"Oh, you did the right thing, Mom."

"I'll never do it again," she said, still feeling sorry. "If I ever need books, I'll go to the public library. I have to apologize to your father."

"You don't have to do any such thing because he's not angry. He was just surprised to see you going straight to Mommy's section. You very much look like her, too, you know," Sheila said.

"Yes, I know."

"So that's why he was disturbed to see you there and—"

"He wants to reopen her case," Anna completed the sentence.

Sheila quickly changed the subject.

"May I ask you how you knew Mommy's book section?"

"I just came here and walked straight to this place without looking. When I looked up, books were there; everyone I like. I was so intent on browsing that I didn't realize his presence," she said.

"Hmmm," Sheila murmured. She was happy to hear that because her thoughts were becoming almost reality now. She was collecting all the facts, thinking that Anna's memory was still here; she just had to realize it. And Sheila would have to be patient. *Daddy can open the case; that's fine, but I'll ask him not to mention anything until she remembers herself.*

Sheila wanted to have things her way without denying her father what he wanted.

"What are you thinking about?" Anna's voice broke in.

"Oh, nothing," Sheila said.

"I think, something," Anna said.

"What do you mean?" Sheila asked.

"I have a feeling that you're disturbed, like your father was."

"Of course not. My thoughts are completely different from that. I have a feeling that you're improving very fast. You just have to realize that, one day…"

"Yes, one day. For now, we're not in a hurry," she said, taking a deep breath.

"Well, as the days pass, you're continuing to improve, so I'm very hopeful."

"But your father is not." Anna laughed a little.

"He's suffering the most without Mom," Sheila said. "C'mon, let's go to the kitchen. I'm hungry." Then they left the library.

Life was normal. Sheila was studying for her exams. Richard had a couple of new patients, and Jimmy was busy with married life. Of course, Anna was taking care of the house, and Sheila never forgot to take notes about Anna's daily activities. She felt that writing those notes was more important than her exams. Dr. Bernard wanted to see the notes every week. Because of all that, she forgot to ask about the police investigation.

"Daddy," she said one day when she remembered, "What's happening with the case?"

"Which case?" He had forgotten, too.

"You wanted to reopen Mom's case."

"Tom wants me to wait until Anna's memory comes back."

"I think so, too, Daddy."

"Then I have to accept everyone's decision, but…"

Sheila understood the hint and took a deep breath.

"But you have to have a little patience, Daddy."

"We have to, but for how long?"

"I think she's improving."

"What's the doctor's opinion?" he asked.

"They're very optimistic," Sheila said.

"Then I think we should wait till the right time."

"We should," Sheila said, lowering her head for a few moments. Then she looked back up and said, "Thank you, Daddy. Thanks very much."

Mr. Scott smiled slightly then put his hands on her shoulders. "We're suffering, surviving, struggling in our way, and hoping for a good result for us as well as for her. So you take care of yourself, of your exams, and of your future. Don't worry. I'm with you all the way." Then he left.

Sheila felt much better after talking with him, but she did not have the courage to ask—*No matter what happens, will Anna be able to stay with us?*

Days passed swiftly for everyone. Although she was very busy, Sheila always had Anna on her mind and in her heart. Curiosity was killing her. She wanted to know everything about this woman she called Mom.

Was she really her mother or not? If not, then what was she going to do with her? Would she let her go with Dr. William? Or would she let her stay? Would her father allow her to do so? *Maybe after I marry Richard, he will let her stay with me.* She asked Richard, and he listened very carefully, and then looked at her innocent face as she stared at him impatiently.

"Sweetheart, you know, you will have full authority about everything, but…" He smiled.

"But what?" she asked quickly.

"Think positive."

"I'm trying—hard, very hard."

"Then?"

"The more I try, the more confused I get."

"Don't think so much."

"Then?"

"Just leave it as is."

"I have to, but what's the solution?"

"The solution will come out by itself."

"How?"

"When she gets her memory back."

"And if not?"

"She will," Richard said. "I told you, think positive. Let's go out. We have to clear our minds."

She started walking with him. But her mind was still on Anna. After a while, she asked, "Where are we going?"

"First we're going outside the hospital, and you tell me, do you want to go home, to go eat something, or to go see a movie?" he asked her.

"To see a movie?" she asked. She forgot her problems momentarily.

"Yes, I watch movies sometimes." He understood why she was questioning him without her explaining. "Why, you don't like to watch movies?"

"I do like to watch, but—" She stopped and lowered her head.

"But what, sweetheart?" he said and he put his hand around her shoulders. "You don't want to go with me?"

She looked at him; saw his face, his loving eyes, which were staring at her; and said very softly, "I'd love to, but—"

He understood her thoughts and said mockingly, "You thought that I'm a doctor and that working is my hobby."

She smiled back and said, "I was so involved in my personal problems that I forgot all my other interests."

He heard her and felt sorry for her as usual but tried to change the subject. "And you know what? We never had a chance to talk about our personal interests."

"I know," she said and looked back up at him. "We started loving each other blindly."

"Yes, we did, and we're still doing that, right?"

"Yes, and always will."

"OK, let's have a good time, just the two of us. Smile, forget all the tension, and have a good time. What do you say?"

"Yes, we can," she said.

"Good," Richard said, holding her hand as they walked toward his car. Then he stopped for a minute. "Sweetheart, could you wait a minute? I have to tell my boss first." He looked at her and smiled.

"Your boss?" She came closer and held his arms with both her hands.

"Yes." He started typing on his cell phone.

Sheila didn't understand. He sent the text, waited a couple of seconds, and received his reply from his boss. He read it very carefully, laughed, and shut his cell phone. "Let's go," he said.

"Richard, where are we going, and who's your boss? Do I know him?" she asked.

"Yes, you know him very well. He's your brother."

"Jimmy!" Sheila exclaimed.

"Yes, we're each other's bosses—we don't go anywhere out of the hospital without informing each other." They both laughed. Sheila sat in the car and closed her eyes. She didn't say a word, and she stopped worrying about where they were going. Richard didn't want to bother her. He sat in the driver's seat, left his jacket in the backseat, loosened and removed his tie, then rolled up his sleeves and started driving. He knew how tired Sheila was, mentally and physically. While he was driving, he thought about Jimmy's message.

> *Yes, you can go. Don't worry about the rest of the day. Take care of my sister. Come home early because three people are concerned about her. Have a good time. See you.*

What a good person Jimmy is, Richard thought.

Sheila moved a little, and said, "I'm hungry," without opening her eyes.

Richard looked ahead at the road and said in a soft voice, "We're going." He had started the car without thinking about where they were going. He just knew they would have a good time. When they were together, thoughts of obligations melted away, and they were very relaxed. While he was driving, he saw a poster for a fast-food place. He stopped the car to see if Sheila was asleep or just relaxing. He touched her very lightly, and she opened her eyes.

"Would you like to have lunch in a fast-food place?"

"Yes—yes. Oh my God, I totally forgot these places—but—is that all right with you?" she asked.

"Oh, I love—this food—sometimes." He smiled at her.

"Let's go, then," she said, opening her door.

They went inside and bought burgers, fries, and soda. He carried the tray of food while Sheila carried the sodas.

"Do you want to sit inside or over there?" Richard asked, pointing to tables outside.

The weather was pleasant, partly cloudy with a light, cool breeze. The restaurant was not very crowded. Sheila said, "I think outside will be better. But—"

"Let's go. I don't like to share my conversation with others," he said, glancing around at the tables inside.

They went outside and sat down at a table for two in the corner. He put the tray in the middle of the table, and she handed him a glass of soda. They sat for quite a while, took their time eating, and talked about a variety of things. They shared their thoughts about almost everything. They decided which movie they wanted to see.

They were both in a very good mood. Richard wanted to make sure that she would like the movie. "We will," she said. "Let's go." Then Richard reminded her that she should let her father know she would be late.

"I'm late all the time—but how late will we be?" she asked.

"I don't know. Maybe let them know that you're with me."

"OK, boss," she said and called her father and gave him a short message for Anna. With Richard, she forgot all her worries for a while. She talked about a lot of different things, asking lots of questions. Richard had to notice she was smart, curious, and knowledgeable. At one point she said she wanted to continue her education but that she wanted to have a little time off after her graduation.

"Why do you want to have a little time off?" he asked.

"To be with you and my parents without any tension. I want to spend time without any worry."

"Good idea," he said.

"I want to be a lawyer," she said quickly.

Richard smiled. "Good to hear that. We need a lawyer in our hospital."

"Really, it will be wonderful. I mean I'll be part of the hospital, too." She looked very happy.

"First be a part of my life—I mean, legally," he said, holding her hands.

"Why? You don't believe me?"

"It's very hard to wait four years." He looked a little disturbed.

"OK, wait a little more, let me finish my exam." She looked at him, and they both laughed.

"Promise!"

"Promise." They started walking. The movie was scheduled to start in fifteen minutes.

"Richard, you forgot your car."

"No, I didn't. The movie theater is right there. We can walk," he said.

"But you're not allowed to leave your car here for more than an hour." She pointed at the sign.

"Really?" He looked in that direction and said, "Thank you. I didn't realize that."

"I know because Jimmy's not here."

"That could be the reason, too." He smiled and moved his car to the pay parking lot.

The movie was very good, and they both liked it. Richard thought it was a wonderful story. "Did you like it?" he asked.

"I loved it," she said.

They left the theater and started walking through the city center, passing all the stores, the museum, the library, the park, and the restaurants that were there.

"Would you like to buy anything?" he asked.

"Not really," she replied. "Would you?"

"I don't think so."

"When do you have time to shop—I mean, your personal shopping?"

"Not grocery—right," he teased her with a smile and put his arm around her.

She didn't fight like she did with Jimmy. She smiled back and looked at him. I mean for your clothes.

"Whenever Jimmy thinks we should go." He looked toward her. "Uncle Tom and Jim are my family. Sometimes I go with Sandra and Jim and sometimes with Uncle Tom. I don't like going here and there without a reason. I don't have the time for that."

"Like right now?" She looked up to see his face to make sure he wasn't passing the time just to please her.

He said, "Not at all. As a matter of fact, I'm having an excellent time. I'm so happy to see how much we have in common."

"Like you're a doctor and I'm not?"

He laughed. "A doctor is a human being, sweetheart. And like a normal person, I want to spend some time with someone who's not a doctor." He squeezed her shoulder then took hold of her hand. "Do you want to go to the museum, or do you just want to walk?"

"Do you like the museum?" she asked.

"Yes, it's a great place to learn."

"I like some museums, but not all of them."

"Let's see if you find this one interesting."

They went inside and walked around. They passed a couple of hours there, until they felt hungry and tired. Richard looked at his watch and asked, "Would you like to have dinner now?"

"It is dinnertime already?" she asked, looking at her watch. They walked to a nearby hotel to get dinner.

The manager saw Richard and approached him.

"Hello, Doc. How are you? Hello, ma'am." He looked at her, then back at him.

Richard introduced Sheila. The manager looked surprised to see Richard alone with a girl.

"I'm very glad to see your fiancée, Doc." Then he looked at Sheila. "This is the first time I've seen him with a girl alone—holding hands. I had wondered how such a handsome doctor could be alone. Then Dr. Jim told me that he was waiting for the right one. And I see right here"—he pointed to Richard and Sheila—"you two will be a wonderful couple. Very good choice, Doc. She's beautiful."

"Thank you," they both said to him.

Then Richard added with a bright smile, "We're very hungry right now. We've had a long walk."

The manager gave them a corner table with a wonderful view.

Sheila sat and said, "Such a nice place and I'm dressed so casually."

"Still looking marvelous."

"Yes, maybe in your eyes." She gave him a loving look with a bright smile.

"Of course. No matter what you wear, whatever you do, you look beautiful—to me."

"Thanks."

"Look at you, you are wearing a very beautiful blouse" he stayed quiet for couple of seconds and then spoke again. "Usually I do not notice these things."

"But you notice my clothes", she said quickly.

"Yes, somehow I am different here—with you."

Sheila stayed quiet for a couple of seconds, staring at him with a smile. Then she said, "I am very happy and proud to be with you."

Richard started to fold his sleeves up while speaking, "I am a simple person. People come to these places consciously preparing and dressing to impress each others."

"You do not have to do all those things," Sheila said. "Your personality, your knowledge and your experience make others impressed."

"Do you think so", he looked at her with his eyebrows up.

"This is a fact," Sheila reply.

The waiter came to take their orders. Richard said, "Today she will order for both of us." He moved his menu toward her, let his head fall back, and closed his eyes.

Sheila smiled and ordered. *He must be tired after all those hours walking around in the museum.* The waiter looked at him with sympathy and left. Sheila looked at Richard, smiled, and started checking her messages. Then she went to freshen up a little. When she came back, Richard was waiting for her. Then he went to wash his hands and freshen up. The food arrived, and Sheila fixed Richard's plate with a little bit of everything. Richard returned, and they started eating. They both were hungry.

"Do you like the food?" she asked just to make sure.

He looked at her. "Yes, very much then he smiled a little " we know each other very well! Don't we?"

"Yes—we do," she replied. The waiter cleared their dishes then brought a plate of dessert, with two spoons, coffee, and cups.

"Thank you," Richard said.

"You're welcome, Doc."

The manager came by and said, "These are from me for the both of you."

"Really?"

"Yes, I'm so pleased that you have such a marvelous companion."

"Thank you very much," they both said.

When manager left, Sheila asked, "Do you come here a lot?"

"Most of our free time—Jimmy loves it here."

They sat for quite a while, talking about a lot of things, laughing and making future plans. Then she looked at her watch. "I think we should go now. You should get some rest."

"Oh yes. I need my bed." They both laughed.

Richard drove Sheila home.

"Thank you very much for all your time."

Richard looked to his right and to his left.

"What are you looking for?" she asked, staring at him with a little surprise.

"Oh, I'm looking to see if there's anyone I'd have a better time with than you."

"You don't have to worry about that. There are plenty of girls who are a hundred times better than me." She looked at him.

"But who do I want to be with?" He looked a little sad.

"What do you mean?" she asked.

"I mean, I spent two years just to convince you and almost another two years to make you say yes."

She looked at him admiringly, then said slowly, "That's not true, Richard. I had feelings for you at first sight—when I saw you treating me in the hospital when I was sick, remember?" She put her hand on his shoulder and shook him a little.

"I remember everything, sweetheart. I do. So why did you ignore me for two years?"

"Because I was scared of losing you."

"I don't understand the logic." He was looking at her with curiosity; a couple of lines furrowed in his forehead.

"I didn't want to be like my parents, to lose each other. I wanted to be with you as a friend. Being with you is the most important thing to me. That's why I suggested that you find a girlfriend or get married. But you got so upset and so sick that I lost control. Then when you offered to sacrifice your eye when I became blind, I realized that I had been selfish. I admitted the reality of my life. And right now I'm with you. I'm sorry that I gave you and myself so many problems." She looked at him, and he gazed into her eyes.

"We had a wonderful day, and now you made my night perfect, sweetheart," Richard said. "I love you. Now I can wait for a couple of months easily." They looked at each other and smiled. "Now please go inside the house."

"Yes, boss. Good night."

"Good night."

He turned his car around and drove home happily.

Mr. Scott was happy to hear that Richard and Sheila had spent some time together. But Anna was worried as she waited for Sheila to return home. She didn't know why she was so worried about her when her father was resuming his regular schedule.

Anna never went into the library after that day, and she was thinking of apologizing to Mr. Scott. She was concerned that because of her Mr. Scott was very quiet and was thinking about his wife. She had stirred up painful thoughts and memories for him. He was focused on his past—his beautiful past —, which had become a disaster because of an emotional argument. He couldn't change the past, but the memories that Anna's presence provoked kept him from moving forward.

What should I do? That question bothered Anna constantly. She should leave the house! But she didn't want to leave Sheila. And if she left, she wouldn't have Dr. Richard's help. *Wherever I go, I'll never learn about my past.* After a lot of agonizing, she decided to stay until her memory came back. *I hope it is soon; I have to know who I am. Why did I become homeless? Why up until now has nobody claimed me? Maybe I don't have anyone. If not, then where did I come from?* These questions swirled through her mind constantly. Sometimes doubts clouded her mind, but she thought, *it's a future, which I want to have; it's my dream, which is not going to happen.* Finally, she decided to apologize to Mr. Scott and get his permission to stay a couple of weeks more. It was her last hope. She would explain to Sheila, too. And when she did leave, she thought, *I'd let Sheila know where I am, and we'll stay in touch.*

That plan helped her to relax. She finished her chores, took her medicine, and went to bed. After a very good sleep, she awoke to a beautiful, clear, bright morning. She felt refreshed. *I feel much better now. I hope the day passes as beautifully as I'm feeling right now*, she said to herself and got out of bed, got dressed, and went into the kitchen earlier than usual. *Today Sheila has her last exam. She's graduating. Let's see, will I attend her graduation or not? Maybe she will not invite me because her father and she miss the woman of the house too much. I can give her that privilege. I couldn't give her anything else. Anyway, I love her, and I'm happy for her success.* Her mind jumped around as she cooked breakfast.

"Good morning, Mom," Sheila said as she came into the kitchen.

"Good morning, honey. Are you ready for the big day?" Anna asked.

"I'm ready!" Sheila said, looking very relaxed. "Do you know that today is my last paper?"

"I know!" she said.

"But how do you know?" Sheila asked with surprise.

Anna laughed. "You only told me ten times," she said, still laughing.

Mr. Scott listened as he stood outside the kitchen. *God, help me; same face, same voice, same actions, and now the same laugh. I think she's my Anna. That woman in the morgue was some mix-up. But the pocketbook, the color of her dress, her hairstyle...I'll talk to Tom again*, he thought.

"Daddy, breakfast is ready!" Sheila called to him. But he didn't have the courage to face her. He kept quiet.

And Anna guessed the reason of his quietness. "Maybe he doesn't want to come here, honey. You're late, so just have breakfast with your father on the porch today."

"Good idea," Sheila said, "but you don't mind?"

"Not at all. We'll have dinner together."

"We will. Thanks!"

After breakfast, Sheila left for her last exam. Mr. Scott said good luck to her and started reading the morning paper. The dishes were still sitting there, so Anna came to clear them. She glanced at him. He was holding the paper in his hands, but his eyes were closed. His head was leaning on the chair. He looked so graceful that Anna couldn't take her eyes away from him for a couple of seconds.

Suddenly Mr. Scott opened his eyes. They both looked at each other. Anna bent quickly to pick up the dishes, and Mr. Scott got up and said, "I'm sorry; I should take those dishes to the kitchen."

"That's OK, sir. I'm sorry to disturb your nap," she said without looking at him.

"I wasn't sleeping; I was thinking something," he said.

"I shouldn't ask, but may I help you?"

"As a matter of fact, you can…but I have to wait."

"I don't understand," she said.

"That's all right."

They helped each other pick up the plates and cups.

"If you have time, I have to say something," she said very politely. She was thinking, *maybe this is how I can help him.*

"Sure, why not?" He said politely.

"I want to apologize for interfering in the library."

"Oh, so that's what you were thinking about? I'm sorry for that, too."

"No, sir; that was my fault. I had a feeling after that that you looked very quiet and disturbed. I apologize for that. I'll never go in there again."

She was talking very fast, and Mr. Scott was looking at her, observing her conversation, her style, and her appearance; everything was the same to him. He said, "May I ask you to sit down?" and he motioned toward the chair.

"I have to take these to the kitchen," she said, looking at the dishes she was holding in her hands.

"That can wait. Please, have a seat."

They both sat facing each other. Anna felt very fresh and relaxed after having a good night's sleep. She was ready for any conversation. She pulled her chair a little closer to the pole that violet lilacs surrounded, spreading their beautiful fragrance.

Both were quiet for a while. Mr. Scott's head was down, and Anna was looking at everything around her: flowers, grass, trees, fountain, lights, gate, and lilacs. Everything spoke to her. She imagined she had decorated everything herself. *I've seen these things before; maybe I've been here for so long, that's why.* She looked to the sky; the sun was shining, and there was not a cloud in sight.

"Very clear," she murmured.

"Yes, it is," Mr. Scott, replied.

"Excuse me?" she asked as she came to her senses and looked at him.

"You were talking about this clear morning."

She realized that and felt a little embarrassed. "May I go now?"

"You may, but I wanted to tell you about my past—at least some of it. Please wait, if you would like to."

"Yes, I'd love to," she said, with the thought, *Maybe in that way he will accept my apology.* She pulled her chair a little closer to the pillar, and the lilacs nearly touched her hair.

Mr. Scott thought, *I should explain to her briefly about my past so she feels free to move around the house. If she's my Anna, maybe it will help her to remember her past.* After a moment, they looked at each other again; Anna moved a little.

"It was four years ago today," he began, "this same date, in the evening, when I came home from work after a long, bad day. That day I had an argument with my superiors because they were stopping me and interfering in the completion of my project, which I was just about to finish. Some of them knew that the project was very good, so they wanted to stop me or make some changes so they could take the credit. I left in the middle of my project and came home. As soon as I entered the house, my wife—her name was Anna, too—Anna Scott," he said, glancing at her. "Her looks, actions, and everything were just like— you. Well, she announced that she wanted to go for a vacation for a couple of weeks, and she didn't want 'no' for an answer. I tried to explain whatever happened in the office, but she refused to hear. 'I'm going ahead with Sheila, our daughter,' she said. 'You can join us.'

"Our marriage was very strong; we had a very good life, the three of us. No one was cheating. She took care of the house and had a part-time job. I was working. We had a daughter in school. In spite of all this, we often had little differences of opinions. We argued sometimes, and most of the time, I wanted to act like the big 'earning man' in the house, and she would give up. But that day she had made her mind up. We ended up in a huge argument, and she left me. I thought, *it's just a threat*, and I said so many things—I don't remember, but whatever I said, I never thought that because of that I would lose her forever. I got my punishment for being rude and stubborn—she left."

Anna suddenly sat up straight in her chair and looked at him very deeply for a couple of seconds. Mr. Scott looked back at her, hoping and praying.

"She left with her pocketbook and nothing else," Anna said sharply. "She just kept walking and walking, without knowing where she was going or what she should do. She was very angry, sad, hurt, and that voice was haunting her: 'this is my house! I'll decide what I should do! She's my daughter; you can't take her!' I'd been feeling I was nothing without my husband, that I couldn't do anything without his permission. I should leave—but where?

"I didn't know, and it was getting dark. A hand came and snatched my bag. I grabbed back. That's all I had—my bag. But that other woman's hand was stronger than mine. We both pulled hard, and I fell to the ground. Oh! I banged my head on something very hard and pointy. I held my head with one hand. I was bleeding. I turned and saw a woman running away with my bag. Then I heard a tire screech, a horn blowing, and a scream, and I saw lots of lights. I remember it was an accident that happened to that woman. I was shaking and dizzy, but I stood up, thinking,

I'll go and claim my pocketbook. I tried to get up but fell again; blood was still running. I saw a car stop in front of me. *Oh God, what next?* I tried to get up but...after that, I don't know what happened." Tears were streaming down her cheeks. She had her arms wrapped around herself.

Mr. Scott stood from his chair and was motionless for a while, completely quiet, staring at her. Then he came to his senses.

"Anna! You're my Anna, my wife! You're alive, here, with me!"

He grasped her shoulders and gently shook them for Anna to stand up. She rose and returned his embrace. Her face was on his chest, her tears wetting him, and he had his face on her hair. He couldn't stop his tears also.

12

Richard was trying to finish his rounds in the hospital so he could get out early and pick Sheila up.

Jimmy was doing the same thing, except that he was worried about her last exam, and he wanted to know how it went. He wanted to have lunch with her and Sandra, if she was available. Sandra usually used her car so she could go see her mother, go to work, or go shopping, but these days Sheila went straight home or to the hospital. He finished all his regular schedules and ran to Richard's office.

"Hey, buddy," Jim, said. He was in a hurry, as usual.

"Yes?" Richard said. He was reading one patient's file in his computer he stopped to look at him. "Are you going somewhere?"

"I have to pick up some papers from someplace; then I thought I would pick up Sheila and drop her off wherever she wants."

"Let's go!" Richard stood up.

"Are you going, too?" Jimmy asked.

"Today is her last paper." Richard smiled at him.

Jimmy understood what he meant. He said, "Oh, go ahead. I'll pick up the papers later; there's no rush."

"Why don't we both go?" Richard suggested, tapping his shoulder. "Brother and—"

"Can we? Brother-in-law...to-be?" Jimmy asked in the same tone.

"Yes, we can."

They both laughed.

"In case of any emergency?" Jimmy asked.

"They will page us," he said. "Besides that, there are so many doctors here, we'll be covered."

Both left Richard's office then went to the main office. They left some important instructions and walked toward the garage. Jim stopped in front of a law office for a couple of minutes to pick up an envelope then came back and wanted to sit in the back so Sheila could sit beside Richard.

"What's the matter?" Richard asked. "Why are you sitting in the back? Are you trying to hide something?"

"I was leaving that seat for sis," Jimmy said.

"Your sister can sit in the back. Come on, take your seat."

When Sheila came out, they both asked about her last exam, and both were happy to hear that it had gone very well. "It's finished, over. I'm a graduate now!" She was screaming, laughing, and tearing up all at the same time.

"What do you want now?" Richard asked.

"What do you mean?" She leaned her face between the two front seats.

"Should we have lunch first, or do you want to go home?" He was looking at her in the mirror.

"Home. Daddy is waiting for me—maybe Mom, too."

"Will you feed us? We're starving," Jimmy said.

"No, I'll never do that."

Jimmy turned his head a little. "Go away. You're too close to me."

She picked up his papers and hit him.

"Ouch, Richard, she's hitting me!" Jim screamed.

She sat back quietly, and Richard kept driving with a smile. "She's your sister; you wanted to pick her up."

"What a mistake!"

Jim folded his arms and sat straight; all three were smiling.

The car pulled into the driveway beside the porch. It was early afternoon, with a clear sky, bright sunshine, and a cool breeze.

As soon as Richard stopped the car, all three said together, "My God!"

They saw Anna against Mr. Scott's chest, and he was holding her and trying to comfort her.

"Another romance!" Jimmy said. "Let's get out of here!"

"I think she got her memory back," Richard said.

"Mommy!" Sheila screamed and jumped out of the car. Both her parents saw her and opened up one arm to reach out to her.

"Sheila, you've got your mother, your *real* one, my Anna," Mr. Scott said. "She's alive, honey! She was with us for so long like a stranger, living like a housekeeper. She's my Anna, Anna Scott, and this is her home. This is our home, like before." All three made a circle. Sheila and her mother were hysterical.

"We should leave them," Jim said.

But Richard said, "Wait a couple of minutes. We're doctors; they might need us."

Sheila totally forgot about them, but Mr. Scott saw Richard. "Son! Come on. She got her memory back; she's my wife, Anna, Anna Scott!"

Richard got out of the car and walked toward them. Anna saw him for the first time as her son-in-law. She gave him a hug; she was laughing and crying at the same time.

"All the credit goes to you, son," she said. She was so emotional, she forgot about calling him doctor, or Richard—just called him son, her daughter's fiancé. "If you hadn't helped me so much, I wouldn't be here. I wouldn't have gotten my memory back, ever," she said as she held him with her other hand. Her one hand was tight around Sheila. Mr. Scott was standing very close to his wife.

Jimmy was still in the car. It was hard for him to decide whether he should leave or stay, but it was Richard's car, so he couldn't just drive off. Someone banged on the car door. It was Sheila. "You're still mad at me?" She said and tried to open the door. Jimmy was excited already.

He got out, and Sheila hugged him. "Today is the happiest day of my life, Brother! Come on, join us!" All five came together, laughing and talking.

"Daddy, how did her memory come back?" she asked, looking at him without any fear or anger. For the first time, she was looking him straight in the eye.

Mr. Scott was in an excellent mood and looked at her with a very bright smile. "She lost her memory because of me, and she remembered everything while we were talking."

"It means she came to talk to you by herself?" Sheila asked.

"She came to pick up the dishes; then she tried to apologize about the library incident. It just came into my mind that if I explained to her a little about my past so she could understand better, she might move around in the house more comfortably."

"That was a very good idea," Sheila said.

"Yes, so I asked her to give me some of her time and tried to explain about my past. I started, and then she came in halfway and started telling the rest." Mr. Scott looked at his daughter and said with an emotional tone, as he was trying to hold back his tears.

"Thanks, honey, for all the effort you put in alone."

"I was not alone; they were there," she said, looking toward Richard and Jimmy. "Oh, I forgot to call Sandra!" She pulled out her phone and started to call. "Sandra! Mommy got her memory back! Come on over," she said very loudly.

Jimmy heard, "…and bring some food, too." Sandra came with a lot of different dishes.

"Oh, I made the lunch; it should be enough for all of us," Mrs. Scott said.

"This is from us as a celebration!" Sandra yelled And Sheila looked at Richard how happy was he.

"Oh my God, we forgot about lunch! It's evening already," Mr. Scott said, looking at his watch.

"Things are very different today. Come on, darling," Mr. Scott said as he held Anna's hand. "We have to serve them today."

The weather was good, a very pleasant evening; everyone was there, in a good mood, excited, and happy. Sheila was over the moon.

Richard was very relaxed and pleasant because he had succeeded with his whole project, especially with Anna's case as well as with Mr. Scott's eye donations and Sheila's mixed-up and confusing life. Now she could think about her future. And Jim was happy that it was finally all over. He was thinking about their marriage, too.

And Mr. Scott's whole life had changed within a couple of hours. When he had woken up that morning, he had thought about his wife, his daughter, her wedding, how he was going to manage everything. Life was very simple and quiet. Anna took care of everything in the house, and he spent his time reading the paper, or in the library, or maybe taking a walk or sitting on his porch. He had a routine, but he felt depressed and lonely, empty on the inside.

Sometimes he tried to calm his mind. *We're in good health, and so far there's enough money for the two of us.* And Sheila had a separate account from his uncle, he thought. But the emptiness was killing him. Over the years, he had learned so many pros and cons, which had made his life miserable. He had gone through so many ups and downs until he finally realized that everybody was equal, their thinking and lifestyles, feelings, and needs. It was too late; he had lost everything—even for a time his only daughter, for whom he had married again. He felt he had lost her. And he realized, *Oh, I was so blind; now I've got my family back. This is another chance for me!* He was rejuvenated. Sandra and Jim were helping him. But Sheila refused to move from her mother's side, and Richard joined them, asking all sorts of questions, increasing his knowledge while becoming part of the family.

After dinner, they sat for a long time. Then Sandra and Jim wanted to leave.

"Shall we go now?" Jim asked Richard.

Richard looked at him. "You two go ahead."

"Good night, and I'm driving your car, you know that," Jim reminded him.

"I know," Richard said.

"Sandra, you didn't bring your car today?" Sheila asked.

"It just so happened that I was late, so Jim dropped me off this morning. I had to take a cab to come here."

"Luckily," Jim said.

"Why?" Sheila asked.

"So I can go home in a luxury car."

"With my pleasure," Richard said and playfully pushed him a little.

Mrs. Scott was listening to their conversation. "Thank you very much, Jim and Sandra, whatever you both did for this family."

"You're very welcome, Auntie," both said one by one with a smile.

Mr. Scott thanked them. "I'll call Tom myself tomorrow, just to give him the good news. OK, son?" He tapped Jim's shoulder and put one hand on Sandra's. "You're my second daughter. Without you, my daughter would not be here." He pointed toward Sheila. "In this situation, thanks are not enough for you two. God bless both of you," he said, and he was getting a little emotional. When they left, Mr. Scott held Anna's hand. "Let's go to the library, darling. We have a lot to catch up on."

"Good night, Uncle, Auntie," Richard said.

"Good night, but where are you going?" Mr. Scott asked.

"I'm staying for a while, then maybe borrowing Sheila's car."

"No," Sheila said quickly. Since she had come back home, she had driven some, but most of the time, Jim, Sandra, or Richard had picked her up. Mr. Scott was so happy to have her back that he had bought her a new car.

Anna knew she didn't want him to go. Mr. Scott said, "Just relax, son. You have a room to sleep in. I think you have to leave early anyway."

"Yes, I think so; I was hardly there at all today."

"Actually, I wanted to talk with you so much, but—
"Anna was saying.

"But not now; today is special," Mr. Scott interrupted, then realized his habit and raised both his hands. "OK, I'm sorry. Do whatever you want to."

Everyone laughed.

Anna said, "Not now; some other time. Good night!"

Richard got up.

"Where are you going?" Sheila asked.

"Home." He looked down.

"This is your home, too," she replied.

"We're not married yet," he said, smiling.

"We will be. Sit down." She tried to pull him, but he made her get up.

"I said we're not married yet."

"Your room is on that side, and mine is here." She pointed to both sides with a smile.

He looked at her. "For how long?"

"As long as we're single," she said.

"Oh, we can marry tomorrow," he said, still holding her hands.

"Too soon." She bent her head.

"But you said it is up to me, don't forget."

"I won't." She was a totally different girl at that moment.

"Let's go then," he said and started walking with her.

"Where are we going?" she asked, confused.

In the garden, on the garden bench, under the moonlight, in the cool breeze and cozy environment, they both sat, side by side. Richard held her hands and said, "Remember when you hid here from me and made me look for you everywhere?"

"I remember. I'm sorry."

"This is not the time for sorry or forgiveness."

They looked at each other. Sheila was puzzled about Richard's intentions. And Richard was trying to make some important commitments.

"This is the time for enjoyment, talking about our future, and making new arrangements," Richard said.

"Which I did already, a long time ago," she said.

"About what?" he asked.

"To be with you," she said.

"I want you to be in my home, my room, with me all the time."

"That can't be possible," she said.

"What do you mean?"

"Because I have a family, and I want to be with them, too." She tried to be serious.

"No one will stop you from doing that."

"Then I can't be with you all the time." She was smiling.

"I think you need some—"

"No, not at all," she said quickly.

"Then listen to me." He held her hands.

"I'm listening." She looked at him.

"I want to marry you," he said.

"Now? It is two a.m." She was in a joking mood.

"I'm going home." He got up.

"How? You don't have a car."

"I'll walk, or call a cab," he said, and he looked serious.

"I'm sorry. I was just joking." She got serious, too. "I know what you want."

"Do you?"

"Yes."

"What?"

"I know, but you can tell me."

"So you want me to propose to you again?"

"Not really. I'm already wearing your ring," she said as she lifted up her hand.

"And still you want me to tell you." He was still standing, but his mood was a little changed.

"No, not really. I just want to make sure."

"Then what do you want to hear from me?" he asked, looking at her.

"That—that…" She was hesitant to explain.

"I want you to be my wife." He stopped for a minute. "Will you?" He was still standing, looking at her.

Something was in his eyes. She held his hands and said, "Yes. Yes, you know that I want that, too. Come on sit down. We can talk about our future."

They sat in the moonlight almost the whole night, talking about all sorts of things, about their future, about the wedding arrangements. Laughing, joking, discussing. And they didn't realize it when the moon got tired and went to sleep before them. Stars followed the moon one by one. And when the new morning dawned, birds started chirping, and they heard some footsteps.

"Oh my, it's morning! I won't get any rest now," said Richard as he looked at his wristwatch.

"Then what are you going to do?" Sheila asked.

At the same time, his cell phone rang. It was Jim, and he said, "Don't worry, buddy. I'll take care of everything this morning. Get some rest."

"But how did you know?" Richard asked, surprised.

"How did I know what?" Jim asked.

"That I need rest," Richard said.

"Because of your being surprised. See, I'm an experienced man." He laughed.

"Thanks, 'experienced man,'" he said as he ended the call. He and Sheila both laughed and went to their rooms for a couple of hours of sleep.

Mr. Scott and Anna Scott did not bother to join them at breakfast because they knew they had been in the garden the whole night, and they would need some rest now. Mr. Scott was very happy after getting his wife back. He wanted to spend all his time with her, at least for a while to catch up on whatever he had missed during those years. He wanted to hear about her difficult life without any of them. Not thinking of anyone except himself or her, not even of Sheila, because he knew she was going to have the best partner in her life.

But Mrs. Scott was a little different. She wanted to know Richard more, everything about him. Sheila was her only child. She had gotten engaged before Anna had her memory back. She wanted to know everything about Richard, his family, his character, and his attitude. She was trying to keep an eye on them to find out how close they were, how much they loved each other. She wanted to know about how they had got together and about their hobbies, their interests, and their planning for the future. Maybe Sheila wants to have more education, and Richard is a doctor. He may want her to stay home, as a housewife. Will she be able to do that? Richard is a very good man. *I've known him since I was in the hospital and in this house, my home; he was always coming here. A couple of times he stayed in the house, too.* And she never detected any tension in Mr. Scott's face. He was always relaxed and happy whenever Richard stayed in the house. *I didn't know about myself, who I was; I never felt any responsibility about anything in this house. But sometimes as a woman and a human, I thought about them. When I saw them together, so happy and relaxed, I felt relaxed, too. But now the situation is different. Now I know about myself, who I am, and that she's my only child. I have to know as much about him as I can.* That's why when they were in the back garden, in the middle of the night, she was a little worried. First, she wanted to interrupt them and ask them to get some sleep. But Mr. Scott was there, too, and he was not concerned about how late it was. *He was trying to know about my past, when I did not have memory. Where was I? How was I spending my life? How many problems did I go through? Wherever I was, what kind of people were there? Was I in danger? And how did I protect myself?* All sorts of questions were coming into his mind, and he was trying to know almost everything.

That's why Anna was watching them through the window while talking to Mr. Scott about her past, which she did not know herself. It was almost morning before anyone would get any sleep.

As usual, they woke up earlier than the youngsters. They came into the kitchen and fixed breakfast for themselves.

As Anna talked with her husband, she felt different, and the questions came automatically.

"And how about you?" She looked at him.

"What about me? I'm alive and well—I survived." He smiled and bent his head.

"Scott, you're hiding something from me," she said as she bent her head to look at him eye to eye. "Your eyes look different. Are you my Scott? Or someone who just looks like him?"

Mr. Scott lifted his head to look at her. "I'm your real Scott, darling. I'm your husband and Sheila's father. This is the same house; everything is the same, except..." He went quiet for a moment.

"Except what?"

"You can read in my face that everything is the same." He was trying to hold the conversation as well as not mention all the sad parts of his life all of a sudden. *She just got her memory back*, he thought.

But for Anna it was very difficult. Now she was curious and wanted to know everything about him, about this house, and about her daughter. What had happened while she was not here? She looked at him and realized his eyes were different. She asked again, "What do you mean 'except'?"

"I went through a lot of problems, darling, without you. I tried to catch one thing, and another would pop up. Surviving is a very difficult and big journey. You did not have a memory—very sad, but God saved you. You did not know who you were; you were just living in the present. But for me—my past and present both were miserable. At that time, to me, my past was a memory, a sad story, and a narrow road of my life I wanted to cross fast.

"But it was impossible to pass. I have a daughter, but she was angry with me. It was impossible to talk to her."

"Why?" Mrs. Scott asked. She was very much in shock, thinking about lots of different things, including Mr. Scott's attitudes and temper. She did not say anything but was very curious to hear more.

Then he told her about his marriage. Why he did it and what had happened after that. How Sandra had given Sheila a place in her house, even though she had been living in an apartment. Luckily Sandra was engaged to Jim, Tom's son. "He was keeping an eye on our daughter, like a big brother. You know Tom?" he asked her.

"Yes, I do," she answered.

"Jimmy became an excellent source for me, through Tom. Every morning, when Jim left for the hospital, I called Tom's house, or sometimes Tom would call me, if anything important or unusual.

"I knew about Richard through them, too. I found out about Richard's love, his sickness, and then one day I got information that Sheila had an accident—she was in the hospital. I could not control myself and went to the hospital. That's where I met Richard. I got a very good impression after meeting with him, such a sober, intelligent, and well-mannered man. When I asked about the payment, he looked at me with empty eyes and said, 'I own this hospital, Uncle. Everything that's mine is hers; she just has to realize that.'

"I was speechless. I felt so proud and happy to hear that but did not say anything. I just said, 'whatever I have is hers, too. I hope she understands.'

"'She will, Uncle. Just give her some time,' he said, and he held my hands.

"I said, 'but now she can't see, so the situation is different.'

"'Nothing will change, Uncle. Everything will be all right, just wait.'"

"I got the important information about eye donations. I went to another hospital, tested my eyes, and got a legal authorization for donating my eyes to my daughter." He looked toward his wife. She was looking so sad, and her face wet with tears. "At one point, I was blind. Yes, I was blind. I had lost my wife, and my daughter whom I could not see was in the hospital. I couldn't help her or comfort her. My job was at risk. I had some savings in the bank. I just gave up, stopped thinking, waiting for time to take me where God wanted me to go. Only Tom knew about this sacrifice. And through Tom, Jimmy found out, then Richard. Both came to me like my own sons. They transferred me immediately to his hospital. Then I found out that Sheila had a successful eye operation and could now see. I was very happy to hear that. I was not able to see, but my daughter got her normal life back, and that was everything for me at that time. They took very good care of me for weeks and also my daughter. Then finally Sheila and I were reunited. She realized how much Richard and I love her. Since then she has been a very good daughter. She came home with me and took care of me and the house, which was completely empty and out of control."

"And where was Samantha?" Anna asked.

"She left quietly because I could not give her attention as a husband."

"But you're still legally married?"

"No, we got divorced very quickly." He looked at her, smiled brightly, and said, "You're still my legal wife.

"Then I had another problem," he continued. "Sheila was engaged to Richard, and he wanted to marry soon. But Sheila was not ready."

"Why?"

"Because she wanted to have my eyes replanted. Then she wanted to finish her college. And in the middle of all that, she found you, and she was very busy and confused because you were so like her mother. All those things were stopping her from getting married."

"Now everything is getting back to normal. We're so lucky," Anna said.

"We're very lucky to be together, along with a son-in-law."

A couple of weeks later were the day of Sheila's graduation ceremony. Happiness was in the air; everybody was getting ready to attend the graduation.

Mr. Scott said to Anna, "I never thought this day would ever come during my lifetime."

"And I was always thinking that I'm a homeless woman who does not have anyone," Anna said, taking a deep breath.

Richard was a different man, laughing, joking, and attending to other activities besides the work at the hospital.

Jim had attended Sandra's graduation last year. But this was Sheila's special occasion.

Sandra was thinking about the last four years, all that she had been through, and thanked God it was over.

And Sheila, since early in the morning, was very busy: What to wear? What to eat? Where to go after the ceremony? She changed dresses and changed again. She kept looking at herself in the mirror and still couldn't decide what to wear.

"Mom, we have to leave early so we can be there on time," she said while trying on a new dress.

Richard arrived way ahead of time.

"You're here already!" she said, surprised.

"Yes, why, am I not invited?" he joked.

He was looking very handsome and graceful. Sheila kept looking at him.

"Is something wrong?" He came right up behind her in the mirror.

"That's the problem," she said.

"What?"

"That—that you look extremely astonishing." She looked at him in the mirror, in his gray suit with a matching tie and combination shirt. He was so tall, with broad shoulders and a very charming face with thick brown hair. He was a very smart and active-looking man, standing behind her with all his charms, position, education, and wealth. But he was also very humble, honest, sympathetic, and kind. She was really impressed with all his qualities.

"Are you talking about yourself or me?" he questioned with a smile.

"About you," she said. "I have to be competitive."

"You are; let's start moving. I hope you don't mind that I'm here so early."

"Are you kidding me?" she exclaimed.

"Then why did you ask?" he questioned.

"Because how come Doc has so much time these days?" she asked, looking at him with open eyes and a bright smile.

"Because Doc knows who needs how much attention, time, and what type of medicine," he said, looking at her in the same way.

"What type of medicine do I need?"

"Medicine of love and attention." He smiled.

"So Doc only knows of giving. Is that right?"

He stayed quiet for a while, and then gave her a long glance. "When docs spend lots of attention, effort, and care, do you know what they get?"

"What do they get?"

"They get back experience, popularity, and attention, plus money and a future."

"Very good! I'm impressed! What are you getting from here?"

"Everything, plus love and a lifetime partner. Is that right?" He looked into her eyes.

"I think you're very much right, plus trust, honesty, faith, sincerity, and sacrifice," she said, getting a little emotional.

"So it's worth it to spend more time," he concluded.

"Yes, but I was thinking about the hospital."

"Your brother is doing very good backup these days, and Sandra is spending more time there, too."

"That means they're not coming?"

"He's your brother," he said. "You should know."

"He will, and I'm going to call him right now." She picked up the phone and started dialing. No one was there. She dialed his cell number no answer. Then she tried Sandra at home. She answered.

"Do you know what day today is?" Sheila asked.

"Friday," Sandra said normally. Maybe she didn't understand.

Sheila got aggravated. "Where's Jim?"

"In the shower." She still didn't understand.

Sheila got more aggravated. "Could you tell him to call me back, please, as soon as possible?"

"Is something wrong?" Sandra asked.

"Yes, there is!" Sheila said, a little louder.

"Oh my God, what's happening now, on your graduation day?" Sandra's voice was louder, too.

"So you remember that today is my graduation?" she asked.

"Of course. What's wrong with you?" Sandra was totally confused.

"What's happened now?" Jim came out of the shower.

"Nothing. It's Sheila. I don't know what she's talking about," she said as she gave the phone to Jim and went to get ready.

"Are you missing me?" Jim asked.

"Of course, and Sandra, too." She wanted to make sure he was coming to the graduation.

"I'll try to do my best, sis. Let me go."

"Don't make me to cry today," she threatened him and hung up the phone.

Richard was watching all her actions, how happy she was, and how beautiful and innocent she looked. It felt as though she never had any problems. *This Sheila is completely different from the past one*, Richard was thinking, and his eyes were on her.

She looked at him and kept looking. She thought, *how graceful he is, and he put all his work and responsibilities aside and is sitting here for me. How lucky I am.* They looked at each other, realized this, and laughed together.

Richard stood up. "Shall we?" He offered his arm for her to take, which she did, and they walked out of the room.

Mr. and Mrs. Scott were ready by then. The four of them left together and reached the ceremony ahead of time.

Students, faculty, and guests were starting to arrive. Sheila had to join her classmates, while guests were seated in reserved seats.

Before the ceremony began, Jim, Sandra, and Mr. Bradley appeared. Mr. Scott asked Tom to sit beside him. Richard sat between Anna and Jim, and Sandra sat next to Jim.

Everyone was happy and excited, and Tom was congratulating Mr. Scott and Anna. Music started playing, and people stopped whispering. The ceremony started. Richard was watching the whole thing thoughtfully. Because of his loneliness, he had a lot of responsibility, and he had been so busy that his own graduation had passed by quietly. This was the second time he was attending one, and he was enjoying every moment. Jim and Sandra were busy taking photos and video. Mr. Scott and Anna Scott were very happy and emotional to see their daughter in a cap and gown. And Tom was observing everything and thinking, *it is a big day. Yes, it is!*

He remembered when Mr. Scott had joined the company. They quickly became good friends; both were very active, ambitious, and hardworking colleagues. Their thoughts were the same. They always gave each other good advice and ideas. They corrected each other and helped each other, too. Everything was so nice. Also, Mr. Scott used to help him whenever he needed it because he was a single parent. Then one day Mr. Scott needed him.

"Tom, I need your help." He had explained everything in a few words. Luckily, Jimmy was home at the time. They both ran; Tom was with Mr. Scott, while Jim was with his daughter, Sheila, who was very sick at that time. Jimmy had just finished medical school; he knew exactly what to do with this partially unconscious girl who was running a very high fever due to shock and tension. He wanted to give her some medicine, but he couldn't decide and called his friend Richard to help him. Richard discussed it with his father, who was pretty sick himself at that time. He heard the situation and prescribed something, which Richard brought himself. He gave an injection because she was unable to take medicine by mouth, and they didn't want her to be awake. Richard came to her house, treated her, and learned about her sad story along with Jim. He had to leave then for his own obligations and responsibilities.

All those ups and downs came to Mr. Scott's life. Tom was thinking, when he suggested to Mr. Scott, "Don't spend your life like me, and don't raise her as a single parent."

"Then what should I do?"

"Bring in a mother for her; it will change your life, too," Tom said.

"Do you think so?" He was doubtful. But Tom encouraged him.

"Yes, look at me. See my son. We have everything except a woman in our lives."

"Well, you will have a daughter-in-law soon."

"Well, God knows when and what—"

Mr. Scott just said, "Think positive. Whatever happened, it is over."

And Mr. Bradley repeated the same thing again and again to Mr. Scott. A couple of months later, Mr. Scott went to Tom and explained about Samantha. "I was happy for Mr. Scott and Sheila," Tom thought. "But after that, Mr. Scott's life was making turns very fast, in sad and zigzagging ways. The last time he came to my house very disturbed, because of Anna, who looked like Anna, acted like Anna, sounded like Anna, but was not his Anna."

"I was confused for a while, too," Mr. Scott said. "It is very difficult to keep the shadow of her whom you love the most in the house; she's here but not yours."

"Then why did you give permission?" Tom asked.

"Because she does not have a memory, and Sheila doesn't want to leave her," Mr. Scott explained.

Then I was puzzled about what to say, except for a few words. "One day Mr. Scott called Mr. Bradley and said he wanted to reopen Anna's death case. I agreed with his idea, but I did not want him to say anything to her and put in her mind that she's his lost wife. We don't know what type of woman she is. Is she playing at being a sick person, or is she really? So Tom told Mr. Scott to wait until she got her memory back, and Mr. Scott listened to that advice.

"'Whatever you say,' he said.

"But inside I was doubtful, too, because Jimmy was saying the same thing. So we reopened the case quietly. The day Jim picked up papers from the detectives' office and went to pick up Sheila with Richard, they found out that she was Mr. Scott's Anna, and she was telling the truth."

Tom's concentration was broken with the announcement, "Sheila Scott." Everyone clapped and whistled. He turned his face to Scott and Anna; both were crying and laughing.

"Congratulations," Tom whispered to both of them. They accepted that. Then the ceremony was over; people started standing up, and some of them were moving already. Richard was with them. He stepped out early to congratulate Sheila first. Tom came out with Mr. and Mrs. Scott once the crowd calmed down and people spread out everywhere. Sheila was half-covered with a large bouquet. Richard had one arm around her, and she was looking like a beautiful doll in her cap and gown. She looked straight at her parents, ran, and disappeared in the arms of her father and mother. Then she hugged Uncle Tom. Richard came slowly to them and stood behind Sheila to make a full group.

"Where are Jimmy and Sandra?" she asked, looking surprised. Jim waved his hand. He was in front of them shooting video. Sandra was taking still photographs. Everyone got together. "Let's have lunch. We're hungry!" Sheila said.

A little while later, they were in a big restaurant at their reserved table. They had their lunch in a very happy environment. They talked, joked, and teased one another. At the same time, Tom was thinking about Richard's future. *He has been doing so much for everyone else. Helping and taking care is his job now, especially since Richard's father's death. Right now is the right time to talk about his future.*

"What are you thinking about?" Mr. Scott asked.

"A little bit about everyone," Tom said.

"That's good. Thank God we're not alone now," Mr. Scott said and Anna nodded her head with a bright smile on her face. She looked very happy and relaxed.

"Do you know, soon Tom will be busy with his grandchild?"

"And I'll be an auntie," Sheila said loudly.

"Yes, of course, and I want you to have your home, too," Tom said to Sheila.

She looked at him. "I have a home," she said.

"Yes—but—" Tom looked toward Mr. Scott and Anna.

"But what, Uncle?"

Tom was looking at her and thinking of how to explain.

Sandra understood and said, "Papa wants you to get married and have your own home. This is your parents' home. Which is yours—but not quite." She looked at Mr. Scott and Anna.

They looked toward Tom, and Mr. Scott said, "We're thinking the same thing about your future, if Richard…" Mr. and Mrs. Scott both looked toward him.

"He's ready," Jim said quickly.

"So is my friend!" Sandra exclaimed.

Richard's face was glowing with happiness, which everyone noticed.

Tom said, "That's it, then. Settle the date."

Mr. Scott and Anna clapped their hands with approval.

"And don't forget to invite Dr. William," Tom reminded them.

"Do you know him?" Mr. Scott looked toward Tom with his eyebrows up.

"We went to high school together."

"Really?"

Tom didn't notice Mr. Scott's surprise and kept talking, saying, "He was a science student, and I was always involved in politics, literature, and writing. When we were in the middle of college, his family moved to another state. Then we both got busier in our lives but never forgot to call each other whenever we had time, and whenever he comes here, we have a cup of coffee together."

"I'm happy to hear that he's your friend; now Scott will join you two, also," Anna said, looking at her husband.

"And how about you?" Tom and Mr. Scott both asked together.

"They're like my second family, especially his wife," Anna said.

"Dr. William is a very helpful man." Tom tried to take his friend's side.

"Yes, he is, but without Mrs. William's help and cooperation, I would not have survived."

"That is true, like without Jim and Sandra, our daughter would not be here." Mr. Scott looked all around.

"Are we inviting everyone without settling the date?" Jim asked while looking at everyone.

Richard smiled and bent his head down. Sheila looked down and started eating.

"Anyway, I have to settle one thing, too."

"I know," Sheila said quickly.

"What?" Sandra asked.

"That you want to have the baby first," Sheila replied.

"Can it be possible, please?" Sandra turned to Richard because she knew he wanted to get married as soon as possible, so she looked at him with hope.

"Look at me. What am I going to do in this condition?" Sandra pointed towards herself.

Richard looked at her and nodded his head and said slowly, "Do not worry."

Jimmy looked at him but didn't say anything because he knew how eager his friend was to settle down, how tired he was of being alone, and how happy he looked now. He turned to Sheila and said, "Sis, I have to say something."

"What now?" She looked at him. Lunch was almost over.

He looked serious. "You're my sister, and you know that!"

"I know; what's new?" She was smiling.

"That I want to be with my buddy." He looked at Richard, who looked very happy and quiet.

"What?" Sheila stared at him and stood up, and so did everyone else.

"I'm serious. You're with Uncle and Auntie now. And I want to be his best man."

Sandra said, "And I want to be her bridesmaid."

Sheila stuck her tongue out at Jim.

"OK, right now we're together; let's take a group pho-to." Jim gave his camera to a waiter.

"Smile, everyone!" Jim looked quickly around everyone.

"It's a happy ending."

The End

ABOUT THE AUTHOR

Amina Haque Sohrawardy is proud to present her debut novel, *Blind.*

Sohrawardy was born in India and was orphaned at the age of eight. She fled to Pakistan and later married and moved to the United States. Throughout her tribulations, she maintained a focus on her education in hopes of getting her writing out to the public one day. She has three daughters and currently lives in New York with her husband.

www.ingramcontent.com/pod-product-compliance
Lightning Source LLC
Chambersburg PA
CBHW050023180626

46810CB00002B/543